CARTEL KILLAZ 3

D1595536

Lock Down Publications and Ca$h
Presents
Cartel Killaz 3
A Novel by *Hood Rich*

Lock Down Publications
P.O. Box 870494
Mesquite, Tx 75187

Visit our website @
www.lockdownpublications.com

Copyright 2020 by Hood Rich
CARTEL KILLAZ 3

First Edition January 2020
Printed in the United States of America

This is a work of fiction. Names, characters, places, and incidents either are products of the author's imagination or are used fictitiously. Any similarity to actual events or locales or persons, living or dead, is entirely coincidental.

Lock Down Publications
Like our page on Facebook: Lock Down Publications @
www.facebook.com/lockdownpublications.ldp
Cover design and layout by: **Dynasty Cover Me**
Book interior design by: **Shawn Walker**
Edited by: **Jill Duska**

Stay Connected with Us!

Text **LOCKDOWN** to 22828 to stay up-to-date with new re-
leases, sneak peaks, contests and more…

Thank you.

Submission Guideline.

Submit the first three chapters of your completed manuscript to ldpsubmissions@gmail.com, subject line: Your book's title. The manuscript must be in a .doc file and sent as an attachment. Document should be in Times New Roman, double spaced and in size 12 font. Also, provide your synopsis and full contact information. If sending multiple submissions, they must each be in a separate email.

Have a story but no way to send it electronically? You can still submit to LDP/Ca$h Presents. Send in the first three chapters, written or typed, of your completed manuscript to:

LDP: Submissions Dept
Po Box 870494
Mesquite, Tx 75187

DO NOT send original manuscript. Must be a duplicate.

Provide your synopsis and a cover letter containing your full contact information.

Thanks for considering LDP and Ca$h Presents.

Hood Rich

Chapter 1

Sandra threw up her hands. Her knees began to shake uncontrollably. She could hear the steady tick, tick, ticking sound coming from the big wooden old school style clock that was perched beside the China cabinet. Her heart raced. She didn't even know that her teeth were chattering until the impact of them crashing together began to hurt her.

Prentice smiled sinisterly and mugged Keisha. "Bitch, you thought you could get away from me? Huh?" he snapped.

Keisha placed his voice almost immediately. Her eyes got as big as saucers. It couldn't be! She questioned her own understanding. Could it be Prentice? How so? She was sure that both she and Mudman had gunned him down all the way back in Baton Rouge, Louisiana. There was no way that he'd been able to survive that barrage of bullets. That made no logical sense.

Keisha took a step back. "Who are you? What da fuck is you doing in my house, mane?"

Prentice was already shaking as he imagined what it would feel like to take the breath out of her body. He pulled the ski mask from his face and slung it to the ground. Keisha's eyes got so big that she felt like her eyelids were going to split at the sides.

"Surprise, surprise." He cocked the hammer and aimed his gun at her.

Keisha grabbed Sandra and pushed her into Prentice. She flipped over the dining room table and took off running. She grabbed her .40 Glock out of her purse as she made her way toward the bathroom. She cocked it and rushed inside.

Prentice took ahold of Sandra and slammed his barrel into her midsection. He pulled the trigger three quick times, watching the bullets exit out of her back. Then he threw her to the floor and popped her twice more. She had been responsible for putting both Mudman and Keisha up. It had been her fault that it had taken him so long to track them down.

He stepped over her and took off running down the hallway. "Arrgh! Bitch, where you at? You just making me mad!" he snapped. He kicked in the first bedroom door that he came to. He slammed it open. He searched it with his eyes. His gun pointed in every direction, looking for Keisha. He came out of the room and hurried to the next door, kicking it in just the same. This room he gave a quick scan. He came out of it and stood outside of the locked bathroom door. "Bitch, come out of there."

Keisha didn't waste time. She aimed and fired at the door immediately.

Prentice jumped out of the way. He landed on the floor of the hallway. He rolled away from the door. "Arrgh! You stupid bitch!"

Keisha kept on popping her gun. She stopped and pulled up the window. With expertise, she slid out of the narrow opening.

Prentice stood back up. He reluctantly peeked toward the bathroom door. "Where you at, bitch?" He jumped back just in case she fired more rounds. When she didn't send any more slugs his way, he stood in front of the door. Through the massive holes inside of the frame, he was able to see her sliding out of the bathroom window. There was a small window directly over the tub. One of her Jordans fell off and landed in the tub. He took a step back and kicked the door in with all of his might.

Keisha jumped from the ledge. In doing so, her gun fell from her waist and onto the ground. She bent over to pick it up. When she looked up, she saw two masked men running toward her from the alley. "Holy shit!" She aimed and fired at them. She watched them duck and scatter in different directions. Then she was running as fast as she could.

Prentice hung halfway out of the window. He busted in her direction, praying that he would hit her. Boom! Boom! Boom! Boom!

Keisha ran in a zigzag formation. She came to a fence in her neighbor's yard and hopped it. The top of the gate cut into her hand, but she couldn't feel it. She was dead set on getting away from Prentice. Her escape, and his capture of her, were the only things keeping her from the heinous death that she was sure he would give her. She still couldn't believe that he was even alive. How could he be? She wondered if she was stuck and running inside of a nightmare. If so, she wanted to wake up so, so badly.

Prentice slipped out of the window and went into hot pursuit of her. With every few strides, he would stop to shoot a slug. When he saw that it hadn't hit her, he grew angrier and kept chase. He wanted to torture Keisha. He wanted to dismember her. He wanted to make her feel as much pain as she'd made him feel, both physically and emotionally. He ran as hard and as fast as he could.

Keisha's lungs were burning. They felt like she had swallowed a ball of fire. She could barely breathe, and on top of that, her stomach began to hurt from the bullets that Prentice had popped into her nearly two years prior. She hopped another neighbor's fence and kept running. Now she was moving barely faster than a jog.

Prentice stopped before he got to the same fence that she had hopped only ten seconds prior and sent three more shots at her. Boom! Boom! Boom!

Keisha ducked and tried to look back. In doing so, she tripped over her own heavy feet and stumbled. She fell to the ground. She scraped both elbows and got to busting at Prentice while blood seeped from her elbows. Her gun let off two shots before it clicked empty. Now she really began to panic.

Prentice hopped the fence. He rushed toward her as fast as he could. Deadly revenge and hatred plagued him. As Keisha was getting up, he was diving forward, tackling her to the ground. She landed on her back. Her head ricocheted off of the ground and bounced forward hard before hitting the concrete again.

She tried to buck Prentice off of her. "Get off of me, you lunatic!" she screamed, and she bucked her hips as hard as she could.

Prentice raised his fist and punched her square in the nose as hard as he could. Her nose burst. Blood came out of both nostrils.

Keisha screamed and head butted him as hard as she could. Her forehead made impact with the tip of his nose, breaking it. She heard him holler. He let off a round, and she slammed her forehead into him again. This time he released his gun. It slid across the grass. Keisha wiggled out of his hold as best she could and jumped up. He kept his grasp on her blouse, ripping it from her frame partly. She broke free and dove for the gun. Her fingers slid around the handle. She turned and got to busting back to back at him. Boom! Boom! Boom!

Prentice jumped up with blood coming down his face and took off running toward the gate. He felt two slugs punch him in the back of the vest. It knocked him forward. He was al-

ready out of breath. Suffering from a cold had both of his nostrils clogged up. The only relief came from when he opened his mouth to inhale. His heart pounded.

Keisha jumped up. She ran toward him, dead set on finishing him off. She got two feet away and aimed at the back of his head. She pulled the trigger three quick times. Click! Click! Click! "Fuck!" she screamed, looking down on the gun.

Prentice, though in serious pain, managed a broad smile. He slowly made his way to his feet. He felt like hot grease had been thrown onto his back, grease so hot that it was able to soak through his skin and into his internal organs. His back was on fire from Keisha's slugs. The bulletproof vest that he wore stopped the full penetration of the rounds, but did very little to prevent the excruciating pain.

Before he could make it all the way to his feet, Keisha rushed him with swinging fists. She was swinging so hard that it looked like she was trying to take his head off. She caught him with two blows in the jaw, then hopped on his back. She could feel the presence of the bulletproof vest. "I hate you! I hate you! I hate you!" she screamed, fucking him up.

Prentice slung her off. He could feel the side of his face bleeding from where her ring had dug into skin. He stumbled backward and caught his balance. His guards went into the air. "Come on, bitch."

Keisha wasn't afraid of him. He'd been whooping her ass ever since they had been seventeen years old. She was used to it, but she knew that his attacks this time would be different. This time he would be trying to kill her, and since that was the case, she was going to make him earn his kill. She rushed him again, swinging fast and hard.

Prentice blocked her first blow. He got caught with her second and third ones, and blocked the fourth. Her fifth landed on his nose again. He fell backward and gathered himself

quickly. He swooped in and wrapped his big hands around her throat. He picked her up in the air and slammed her to the ground so hard that he knocked the wind from her body. She curled into a ball on the pavement and struggled to breathe. Prentice grabbed her by the hair and pulled her up. She swung weakly. He blocked it and head-butted her as hard as he could, knocking her out. She slumped to the ground. He took a step back, breathing heavily. He looked down on her, and a million thoughts seemed to rush through his mind at once. He wanted to kill her right then and there, but he was without a weapon of choice. He had visions of gutting her like a deer. He wanted to enjoy murdering both Mudman and Keisha. They had scarred him for an eternity. When he took them off of the earth, it had to make him feel vindicated. There was no way around that. He grabbed a handful of her hair and yanked her up, slamming her against the back of the house.

"Bitch, where is Mudman? I wanna kill both of y'all to-gether."

Keisha was in another world. Her eyes were rolled into the back of her head. She wasn't lucid. She slumped to the ground again.

Prentice picked her back up and slammed her against the wall. He smacked her so hard that his hand was still vibrating when he pulled it back. "Where is Mudman?"

Keisha woke up with tears in her eyes. She felt the stinging slap. Slowly, her eyes began to focus. When the image of Prentice became visible, she frowned. She thought about his question. "Nigga, fuck you. You got me, now kill me. Kill me, and get dis shit over wit'. Pussy!" She hocked and spit into his face.

The loogey caught Prentice in the right eye and oozed down his cheek. He lowered his head. It dripped off of his chin onto the concrete. His anger shot through the roof. He head-

butted Keisha, knocking her back out. He picked her up over his head with psycho strength and slammed her to the ground as hard as he could with every ounce of force he could muster. She landed on her neck. It cracked, then she lay flat on the ground, unmoving.

One of Prentice's hittas rushed into the backyard. He held a choppa in his hand. "Bruh, we gotta go. Ma'fucka spotted Twelve not too far away. Let's get up out of here," he called.

Prentice nodded. "Bring my whip around." He tossed him the keys.

The hitta caught them. "A'ight. I'll be back." He took off running.

Prentice stood there for a moment. He looked down on Keisha and clenched his teeth. He kicked her in the ribs. She flipped over and winced in pain. "Get yo' ass up. Get up!"

Keisha forced herself to move. She was in so much pain that it was killing her. She stumbled just a bit. She landed with her back against the house. It felt like every portion of her body hurt. Tears of agony eased down her cheeks. "What do you want from me?"

Prentice leaned into her face. "To gut you next to Mudman. Bitch, I already took yo' baby, and dat wasn't enough for me. I took yo' sister Kayla. Dat ain't do shit for me either." He snickered. "When I murdered Kimmie, dat made me feel some type of way, but it wasn't enough. It gotta be you. It gotta be you, next to Mudman. I'ma ask you one last time. Where is h---?"

Keisha kicked him as hard as she could in the nuts. She kicked him so hard that she fell on her back. She watched him fall to his knees and onto his side, grunting in pain. She took off running for dear life.

Prentice's young hitta rushed into the backyard at the same time Keisha hopped over the back fence. He took off running

behind her. "Hey! Bitch! Stop!" He jumped the fence and broke camp, gaining on her.

Keisha hopped another fence. She fell to her knees and let out a whoosh of air. Then she jumped up and ran into the alley. She could hear the police sirens screaming five blocks away. She sprinted down the alley. She saw Prentice's car parked in the middle of it. The front doors were wide open. There was smoke coming from the exhaust. She prayed that another one of his soldiers didn't jump out at her. She was out of breath and felt weaker than a child. When she got to the car, Prentice's hitta stopped in the alley and knelt down. He cocked his assault rifle and let off spray. Boom! Boom! Boom! Boom! The bullets ricocheted off of the car. Sparks flew from them.

Keisha ran and hopped into the car through the driver's door. She threw the car in drive, stepping on the gas. This wheels spun, kicking up gravel. Then she was storming out of the alley as the back window shattered. Prentice's hitta continued to chop at the car. She peeled off into the street and scurted down it as fast as the car could take her. Her face was full of blood. She felt dizzy and panicked. All she could think about was making it to Mudman. Mudman would figure everything out. She was sure of this.

Chapter 2

Figgady stood over Chiah's grave with tears pouring down his dark-skinned face. He couldn't believe that his baby girl was gone. She had only been six years old. It was way too early. He kept telling himself that it was his fault, that had he never bought her to Baton Rouge from Chicago, she would still be alive. He hated himself for allowing his baby to get caught in the crossfire of Prentice's deadly wrath. He lowered his head and rubbed her tombstone.

"Damn, I miss you already, Princess. You betta know that he will never get away with this. Daddy got you, baby. I'ma burn this clown, and then I'm coming to you, baby girl. I promise." He placed his thumb and forefinger in the crevice of his nose and broke down.

Pistol stood a safe distance away. He felt just as horrible. He didn't like southern niggas already. Based off of what Prentice had done to Figgady's daughter, he felt that the killas in the south were cowards. He felt they preyed on the weak, things that he would never do himself. He had a sadistic side to himself, but he could never fathom what it would take to get him even close to doing to anybody what had been done to Chiah. He couldn't wait to enact Figgady's revenge. Whatever his right hand man was 'bout he was 'bout that life as well.

Figgady kissed Chiah's tombstone and rubbed over her name, which had been chiseled into the stone. "I love you, baby. Like I said, Daddy'll be there soon."

Pistol stepped beside him. "Nigga, you ready to make dis trip out to da west coast?"

Figgady stood up and nodded his head. "Yeah. I ain't got shit down here no mo'. That nigga Prentice gotta feel dis pain, homie. Ain't no ma'fucka gon' take my shawty off dis earth

and not answer for what dey did. Let's mount up. I done already linked up with my cousin Pooty out dat way. He over in Los Angeles. But from what he telling me, dat ain't nothin but a short drive away. We gon' station at his trap and holler at Oakland from a distance."

"What about Mudman? Dat nigga answer his phone yet?" Pistol asked.

"Fuck dat nigga too. If he would have arranged to meet up sooner, Chiah would still be alive. Far as I'm concerned, he in the same boat right along with Prentice. Both of dem niggas can get it." The thunder roared over the dark graveyard. It smelled heavy with the scent of rain. An electric lightning bolt illuminated the sky.

"Dat's all I wanted to know. Seem like if one of da homies going through something dis serious, a ma'fucka should at the very least be here to send his condolences in person. But if it's fuck him too, then dat's just what it is."

Figgady looked back down on to Chiah's grave. Rain began to descend from the sky. He closed his eyes and fell back to his knees. His forehead rested against the cool stone. "Don't no ma'fucka in dis world have any idea what I'm going through right now. All I can see is murder. Dese niggas finna pay. Dat bitch too. Fuck it. Everybody from that circle can get it in blood. On my mama."

"Hold his hand out straight. I'm ready to fuck a ma'fucka up 'bout trying to short change me!" Mudman exclaimed, stepping into the trap house's kitchen. "Y'all gather around dat table, and don't a muthafucka move. I catch anybody moving, and they taking the discipline chair next." He pulled the

meat cleaver from the rack and came back into the living room.

Greg sat in the chair naked. He shook as if he was fresh out of water and it was freezing cold outside. "Mudman, I swear it ain't come up short on my end. I been weighing everything just like you showed me how. I think dis kilo was just a few ounces short." He trembled.

Mudman brushed through the crowd. He slid Greg's hand under the wooden board, and held it by the wrist. He nodded at Ashley. Ashley stepped out of the hallway and pinned her shotgun on the back of Greg's head. She'd been working under Mudman for six months. She knew how he got down. He didn't accept excuses. He stuck to a playbook that he refused to step outside of. She knew her orders were simple. If Greg tried to get up from the table while Mudman disciplined him, she was to pull her trigger right away. She already had her mind set on splashing him. "Greg, if I was you, nigga, I wouldn't move." The Game was the Game. She was simply a player inside of it, a player that Mudman controlled with his mental joystick.

"Damn, Ashley, it's like that?" he asked the high yellow female hitta.

"You heard what I said."

"Y'all shut the fuck up," Mudman ordered.

The pair grew silent. The two-story house was so quiet that they all could hear a roach crawling across the wall. They were well aware of Mudman's rap sheet. They knew he had a bunch of bodies under his belt, bodies of both male and females. That meant that the entire room was in jeopardy.

Mudman leaned into Greg's face. "You two zips short on dis kilo. That's fifty-six grams. Sixteen hunnit dollars. Or in yo' case, yo' life if you don't come up wit' my shit." Mudman

set the meat cleaver on the table beside Greg's hand. "You got somethin' you wanna tell me?"

Greg slowly shook his need. "I would never come at your shit bogus like dat, Mudman. I respect Payroll too much."

Mudman frowned. "Payroll? What da fuck Payroll gotta do wit' dis?" he snapped.

Greg began to shiver. "Look, man, everybody know that Payroll put you on. Dat's why so many niggas go hard for you. They respect you because in doing so they are actually honoring Payroll too. Payroll was the heart of Acorn."

Mudman mugged him. He didn't give a fuck about Payroll. In fact, Mudman had been the reason Payroll had been assassinated in the county jail. To him, Payroll was a rat. A chump. A low life. He didn't respect him or his legacy. "Is dat so?" he asked, picking up the cleaver.

Greg nodded. "Yeah, big homie. So what the fuck would I look like stealing from Payroll? I got too much loyalty in me to be doing something like that."

"Hold his shit," Mudman ordered as he watched his bodyguards pull Greg's fingers apart on the chopping block.

"What the fuck, Mudman? Why don't you believe me?" He watched the blade whip through the air in a downward swipe. The next thing he felt was the big blade slicing through both his skin and bone. The tip of his finger slid across the table. Blood squirted from the digit. It shot across the chopping board and along the table. Greg hollered as loud as he could.

Ashley slammed the shotgun into the back of his head. "Nigga, shut yo' bitch ass up," she ordered. She tried not to look at the top of his finger that was in the middle of the table.

Greg bit down on his bottom lip. He tried his best to contain the agony that was screaming from his digit. He squeezed

his eyelids tight together. His feet stomped at the ground. "What the fuck, Mudman?"

Mudman picked up the half of finger and stuffed it into Greg's shirt pocket. "Dat's one down. Nine to go. Nigga, you missing two zips. Where is my shit?"

Greg shook his head. "Mudman, I ain't got yo' shit. I'm sitting in dis ma'fucka naked like everybody else besides you and these shooters. Why the fuck would I even think about some shit like that?"

Mudman slammed down the cleaver so fast that everybody in the room jumped when the loud sound of the blade making contact with the chopping board resonated around the house. Mudman wiggled the handle, chopping Greg's middle finger all the way from his body. "Answer my muthafuckin' question."

Now Greg was hollering so loud that it could be heard outside of the house. Sweat poured down the side of his face. He was ready to cry. "Mudman, please don't do this shit to me. I got two li'l girls. I would never do anything to jeopardize my family," he said, looking up at Mudman. "You should be checking on her."

Mudman stood up. He peered over at Ashley. "What you saying? You saying she got somethin to do wit' my dope being missing?"

Ashley tensed behind the shotgun. "No suh. I been working for you for six months, Mudman. Ain't shit ever came up short on my watch."

Mudman looked back down to Greg. "You got somethin' you wanna tell me?" He pulled another one of Greg's fingers out toward him.

Greg whimpered like a frightened little girl. "Mudman, just let me give you the sixteen hunnit. I mean, I ain't got it

right now, but I can get it for you. You ain't gotta cut off no more of my fingers. Please, man."

Mudman raised the blade and sliced off the third finger. This one squirted three times. It added to the other blood that had puddled in the center of the chopping block. The blood pooled and wound up dripping off the side of the table and onto the linoleum floor.

Greg was shaking in his chair now. He could no longer contain the pain. His back was full of sweat. "Mudman, dis wasn't my idea. I would never steal from you. Blame it on dis bitch." He nodded his head back into the shotgun.

Ashley tensed up. She looked past his head into the gray eyes of Mudman. "Don't believe this lying son of a bitch."

Mudman held his thumb. "Bitch nigga, keep talking," he ordered.

Greg was shaking like crazy. "She stole yo' dope, Mudman. She been stealing from you for the longest. Little by little. Dat's how she been paying all of her bills."

Ashley's pretty face turned into a scowl. "Oooh, let me kill dis nigga, Mudman. He lying on me. How could any real man lie on his daughter's mother?" she questioned.

Mudman raised the cleaver. "You say she got my shit? Huh? You sho' 'bout dat?"

"Yes! Yeah, man, fuck, I swear to God I am!" Greg shouted.

Mudman took a step back. "Where den?"

Greg was shaking like crazy in the chair. Sweat dripped off of his chin on to his chest. It looked like he'd just gotten out of the swimming pool. "Soon as she steals it, she sells it," he said. "She probably got dat li'l two zips on her right now. Seeing as you don't make yo' shooters strip down." He swallowed his spit. "I would never be going through dis shit if Payroll was free," he blurted.

Mudman's eyes got bucked. "Aw, dat's what you thank? You thank dat nigga be letting you steal from him? Den sit back while you blamed dat shit on yo' baby mama?"

"What?" Greg asked, dumbfounded.

Mudman took a step back. "Bitch. Blow his shit. Now!"

"Wait!" Greg tried to jump up from his seat.

Ashley pulled the trigger of the big double barrel shotgun. Both rounds ripped into Greg's jaw and took his face partway off of his head. Two gaping holes appeared. His brain matter seeped out of the holes and onto the carpet. Ashley stood back with the smoking gun. She felt no remorse. Greg had tried to throw her under the bus, and she was thankful that Mudman had seen right through that shit.

Mudman slid the black latex gloves onto his hand. He knelt down and flipped Greg on his side. He yanked his right ass cheek apart and pulled the plastic bag containing his two ounces of dope out of him. He stood up. "Y'all see dis shit? Huh? Don't shit get past me. I don't trust a soul in dis room. None of you. I respect all of you until you try me like dis." He looked from face to face. The onlookers appeared shocked. He tossed the plastic bag on the table and took his gloves off. "Get rid of dis ma'fucka, and bag them zips up." He walked into the kitchen. "Ashley, come here, shawty.

Ashley stepped over Greg's body and stepped in the kitchen. She watched Mudman wash his hands in the sink. "Yes?"

"Shawty, you know a ma'fucka jam wit' you da long way. I ain't believe none of that shit coming out of dat nigga's mouth. You hear me?"

She nodded. "Yeah, I hear you. I appreciate dat too."

"It's cool. Go on back in dere and help clean up dat mess. Oh, and Ashley?"

She stopped and turned around. "Yep."

"Shawty, don't thank it's sweet. You fuck up, and I'ma buss yo' brain. Dat just how dis shit go, ya feel me?"

She smiled. "I already know, Mudman. Can I go now?"

Mudman looked into her green eyes and felt odd. His eyes coursed up and down her body, even though he didn't mean to. Ashley was 5'5" tall. She weighed 135 pounds. She was light-skinned, mixed with Italian and Black, with green eyes and slight dimples. She was gorgeous. Mudman tried his best to ignore that fact. "Yeah, shawty, go on 'head."

Mudman's phone vibrated. He pulled it from his pocket. He read the text from Keisha. It read: "Prentice alive. He tried to kill me. Where are you?"

He felt like he'd lost his breath. He called her phone immediately. He knew that he had to be tripping. There was no way that Prentice was still alive.

Chapter 3

Two months later...

Mudman handed Mars a bottle of pink Sprite. It had ten ounces of pure codeine inside of it. Mars took the bottle and shook it up before twisting off the top and downing the liquid in big gulps. He took the contents all the way to a third of the bottle. Once there he burped and covered his mouth after the fact. "Damn, my fault, big homie. It feel real good to be up out of that though," he said, adjusting himself in the passenger seat.

"Yeah, who would have thought they was gon' keep yo' ass for a li'l minute before they released you?" Mudman kept rolling the Bentley truck. The soft leather felt good to him. He struggled to keep his eyes open.

"Homie, you know how dat shit go. I go in there for one thang, and they wind up keeping me for a whole 'nother one. It is what it is. That shit behind me. I'm ready to get out here and get to dis money though. What you got lined up?"

Mudman continued to cruise down the avenue. He had a truck of hittas following close behind him, and another truck directly in the front. Each vehicle had four men inside. All of them were strapped. Mudman didn't believe in arming his crew with anything less than fully automatics. He felt if it was time for them to get it in that they would be able to spit rapidly at all times. He positioned the Draco on his own lap. He scanned the streets through his Chanel glasses.

"Before we get into all dat, I just wanna let you know that I appreciate you for knocking Payroll's bitch ass off and for crossing all the way over to me. Trust me, it's gon' be well worth it. Know dat." Mudman turned up the volume to Kevin Gates's new album. He nodded his head.

Mars looked into his rearview mirror as they strolled through the nightlife of Oakland. It was eighty degrees outside with a light summer breeze. The day was Friday and Mars was happy to be home. "Say, potna, since when Ashley move up in ranks like dis?"

Ashley sat in the far back seat of the 2020 Bentley truck. She had half of her face covered with a black mask. Her pupils were dilated because of the two capsules of pink Mollie she'd taken thirty minutes prior. She held an all-black Draco. Her attention was out the windows. She scoped the streets to make sure that they weren't caught off guard. Her window was rolled down low enough so she could stick the barrel of the assault rifle out of it. If anybody got to shooting at them, she would easily be able to retaliate immediately. Mudman had already given her the order to shoot to kill. She was confident that she would do exactly that.

"Nigga, don't start dis shit wit' me. Yo' ass ain't even been out for ten hours and already you finna do dis?" she questioned.

Mars smacked his lips. "Bitch, who the fuck you talking to?"

Ashley laughed. "Mudman, wit' all due respect, get yo' guy. Please."

"Shawty, I don't do no ma'fuckin' saving. You already know how dis shit go. You wanna check dis nigga, den be my guest. Only the strong survive around here," Mudman said, rolling into Acorn Projects.

Mars turned around to look at Ashley. "Bitch, you already know what it is. You ain't finna check me, not now, not ever. You betta thank about my ma'fuckin' body count," he snapped.

"Nall, nigga, dis ain't what it used to be. You betta question about mine. Since yo' ass been in dat county, I done

passed you up. You keep coming at me like you all dat, we finna have a major problem. Know dat."

"Bitch, what?" Mars looked over at her, and then to Mudman. "What's dis shit about? When hoes start sitting in the main whip up front?"

"She been paying her dues. Shawty real trustworthy and efficient. She ain't lying 'bout her body count neither. She been laying ma'fuckas down like a daycare worker. Don't just anybody get to roll up front with me." He looked into his rearview mirror. He and Ashley locked eyes. He held hers for a seconds and then looked off.

"Say, Mars, I don't know what yo' problem is wit' me, but whatever it is, you need to let that shit go fast. I'm all about dis Blood Thirsty shit. Trust and believe that, and I'm first after Keisha. You gon' find dat out real quick." She rolled her eyes and went back to looking out of the window on security.

"Yeah, dat's what I was finna ask you. What Keisha think about all dis?" Mars asked.

To Mudman, Mars sounded like a jealous sucka. He couldn't believe how bitch made he was acting. "Nigga, don't worry about how my bitch feeling about my operation. I got my house in order. Now that you home you can jump on dis Blood Thirsty shit, or you can kick rocks and go fuck wit' da other side before we blow dey ass."

Mars was offended. "Fuck you mean by dat?"

"You heard what da fuck he said, nigga. Get yo' mind right or beat it. Dis ain't dat Payroll shit no more. We under Mudman, get yo' ass in line," said Ashley.

Mudman turned around to face Ashley. "Say, shawty, shut yo ma'fuckin' mouth before I pop you in dat. You hear me?"

She nodded. "Yes, daddy. I hear you."

Mars eyes were bucked wide. "Daddy?"

"Nigga, everythang she said is the truth. Dis ain't no Pay-roll operation no more. I'm the king. Oakland is mine. You gon' get jiggy wit' dat shit, or you gon' go to the other side. Which is it gon' be?" Mudman snapped.

Mars sat there in silence. He looked from Mudman to Ash-ley. He felt a serious case of anger and disrespect. He didn't like how Mudman was talking to him as if he was a nobody. He demanded respect from all men. He didn't give a fuck who Mudman was now. And when it came to Ashley, he didn't feel that any female should be able to talk to any man like that without being fucked over. He wanted to kill her. But he knew he had to be smart. He was broke. Mudman had the key to the streets. He needed him. He would do whatever he had to in order to gain his trust. As soon as he had it, he had plans on fucking him over in the raw.

"Say, Mudman, I'm riding wit' you, big homie. Dat's my bad. Say, Ashley, I apologize, shawty. It's all love."

Ashley grunted. "Nigga, it's good. You just need to fuck somethin so you can mellow out. Lucky for you it's finna be plenty hoes at yo' welcome home party. Some of the baddest bitches in Oakland. I made sure of that." She smiled under her mask and went back on point.

Mars sat back in his seat, fuming. "Yeah, well, I hope so. I definitely need to release some of dese pent-up frustrations."

Mudman pulled into a parking space in front of Acorn's headquarters. Before he cut the ignition, his parking space was surrounded by ten of his shooters. They made sure that the coast was clear for him to step out of the whip. Behind them were the sounds of Lizzo beating out of the speakers of the Projects. The parking lot was crowded with cars and trucks. Mudman stepped out of his truck. Ashley stepped in front of him with her Draco. Her eyes were lowered to slits. She scanned the atmosphere, hungry for a rival.

Mars stepped out of the truck. He could smell the Ganja in the air. "Mane, let's get off in dis I so we can see what it do.

Twenty minutes later, Mars had his head tilted sideways while he tooted a half gram of Sinaloa off of a mirror that was on the table in front of him. He finished and pulled his head back, pinching his nostrils closed. The drug rushed through him immediately. When he opened his eyes, the drug had taken its full effect. He closed his eyelids again. He felt the numbing sensation all over him. It felt like he was floating on air.

Ashley stepped into the room with her arm around the shoulders of two Puerto Rican women. Both had long curly hair with dark makeup. Their bodies were well put together. Ashley cleared her throat. "Uh-um!"

Mars was in the middle of a nod. He opened his eyes to see the three dimes standing in front of him. He looked them up and down and straightened up on the couch. "Damn, shawty, who is dey?" He noticed that one of them had nice-sized breasts while the other had small ones. Both looked incredible to him.

Ashley smiled. She had her natural long hair dropped down her back. Her green eyes popped in the dimly-lit room. "Dis one to my right is Sari." She was the one with the bigger breasts. "To my left is her sister Ari. They're twins, and they wanted to meet you." Ashley rubbed all over their asses. "They supposed to graduate high school this semester. Maybe before they do, you can show 'em what's really good?" She looked back and forth between both girls. "Ladies, show 'em those asses."

They turned around. Both girls had on tight skirts that hugged their asses. Ashley's hands yanked up the material to expose their thongs underneath. Mars saw their light brown cheeks, and he felt his piece stir.

Ashley smiled. "I'll leave them with you." She slid from the back room and closed the door.

Mars sat upright. "Shawty, y'all look young as hell. Are y'all grown?"

Sari stepped forward and knelt down beside him. "Damn, nigga, what, you da police or somethin'? Ain't nobody worried about all dat right now." She rubbed her hand over his crotch and found his erection. She unzipped his pants and pulled it out, stroking it in her fist. "Is it true that you finna be one of the manor bosses in Cokeland?" Cokeland was what those deep in the slums called Oakland because the city was infested with narcotics.

"Hell yeah, shawty. I can't see it no other way."

Sari licked around his head. "My mama always told me to never get on my knees for a nigga unless he was a major one, or about to be a boss. Seem like it's okay for me to do dis then." She sucked Mars into her mouth and deep throated him like a professional.

Ari kissed along his neck. "Dat feel good, what my sister doing to you? She know how to suck a dick, don't she?" She trailed her tongue along his neck until their lips were all over each other.

Mars slid his hand under her skirt and over her panties. Her pussy beat against his fingers. She felt hot and wet. "What you know how to do?"

Sari sucked him faster and pumped him in her fist at the same time. She squeezed her thighs together. Her pussy was already seeping juices into her panties. She couldn't wait to fuck Mars. She'd heard a lot about him, and she felt that if she

and Ari could get their cats on his pole, then they could lock him down for future reference. Having a boss in your corner was half the battle of surfing for a woman in Oakland, her mother had always told her.

Ari dropped down and pulled his dick out of Sari's mouth and slid it into hers. She sucked him tighter and faster. Her hands rubbed all over his stomach as he laid back and received her pleasure. She popped him out. "You like dis, daddy?"

Mars groaned in response. He slowly humped upward into her mouth. "Fuck, shawty."

Sari slipped her panties down her thighs. She stepped out of them and placed her right foot on the couch. She rubbed her cat in Mars's face. "You want some of dis young pussy? Huh? You think you can handle it?"

Mars pulled his piece out of Ari's mouth and positioned Sari over it. He held his dick in his fist. The head rubbed up and down her slit. Her crease felt damp and hot.

Sari grabbed his pole and slid down on to it. Her eyes rolled to the back of her head. She grabbed the back of the couch while she rode him slow at first. Gradually, she began to pick up speed. "Unn. Unn. Unn. Shit. Oooh. Unn. Mars. Daddy."

Mars held her big ass while she bounced up and down, taking him like a pro. "Damn, baby. Huh. Huh. Huh. Huh." He got to slamming her down hard on his pipe, fucking up into her from the couch.

Ari came and released Sari's titties from her bra. "Suck on 'em, Mars. I love to watch Sari get her breasts sucked." She sat on the table in front of them with two fingers deep in her pussy. When Mars sucked on Sari's nipples with his thick lips, Ari sped up the pace on her fingering. This sight drove her crazy. She wished that her breasts were as big as her sister's. Since they weren't, she loved to watch her get them sucked.

Sari popped her hips forward at full speed. She grunted with each forward thrust, and shivered every time Mars sucked hard on her nipples. His piece was stretching her to capacity. It kept feeling better and better to her until she couldn't take it anymore.

"I'm finna cum! I'm finna cum! Aw fuck!" she screamed, and came all over Mars's thrusting penis.

Ari fell to her knees and sucked Mars's sack while he continued to plow into Sari. She grabbed his pole out of her and slid it into her mouth. She sucked him deep and fast.

Mars pushed Sari off of him and grabbed Ari by her hair. He slung her over the couch and slid into her from the back. She was so wet that he was able to slip into her easily. He took ahold of her hips and got to fucking her at full speed. Her box was slightly tighter than Sari's.

"Oh! Oh! My Gawd! Gawd! Shit! Shit! Shit!" she screamed, holding the back of the couch.

Sari smacked Ari's ass cheeks and squeezed the meat there. She thought that Ari was so strapped. She wished that her ass was as round, big, and perfect as Ari's was. She was obsessed with the size of it. "Fuck her, Mars. Fuck her as hard as you can. Wit' all dis ass, she can take it." She slid two fingers back into her gap and worked them as fast as she could while she watched Mars pound Ari out.

Mars yanked Ari back to him and sucked on her neck while he remained planted deep within her womb. "You bitches finna belong to me. You hear me? Both of y'all finna belong to me!" He went into overdrive, grunting and fucking as fast and as hard as he could with no mercy. A steady clapping sound could be heard as their skins slapped into each other.

Ari screamed. She slammed back into Mars four hard times and came, falling forward. Mars continued to fuck her

as hard as he could. Her head bumped into the back cushions of the couch whole he did his thing.

Mars saw Sari come over and open Ari's ass for him. Ari's rosebud peeked at him, and the sight was too much. He imagined entering into her crinkle back there and came hard. He pulled out and nutted all over her backdoor and ass cheeks. Sari licked it off of Ari's ass, moaning with her fingers up her box.

Mars fell off of her. "We finna set this shit in stone. You li'l hoes finna belong to me. Mudman gotta let me have y'all."

Both girls laughed.

"Shit, long as you finna be getting dat bag and you can afford us, den we wit' it," Sari said, rubbing his abs.

"Yeah, wherever my sister go, I go. Dat's how that work. If Mudman say it's cool, den we yours."

"Aw, don't worry about dat. I'm getting you hoes one way or the other."

Hood Rich

Chapter 4

Figgady sucked the barbecue sauce off of his fingers and grabbed his glass of pink lemonade that he'd dropped three capsules of Mollie into. He downed half of it and burped.

Pooty nodded. "My shorty be putting dat shit down, don't she?" Pooty was six feet even, dark-skinned, with brown eyes and a heavyset frame. He had a low cut with waves.

Figgady nodded and scooted away from the table. "She a'ight. What's good wit' dis money, doe? I need to get my bag up before I go at dis nigga chin. I heard Prentice done took a strong hold of Crenshaw already. I don't know who the fuck he know up here, but if he caking like dat already, den dat means his weaponry gotta be way up to par." Figgady took another sip from the glass.

Pooty brushed off the comment about his baby mother Linda's cooking. He knew she could throw down. He didn't give a fuck what his cousin Figgady was talking about. "Nigga, I done already told you. We finna hit Amigo n'em about fifteen blocks over. Word on the street say they just got a big shipment of that crystal shit in earlier this morning. They probably been breaking that shit down, and bagging it up all afternoon. Dat's all everybody around dis ma'fucka fuck wit'. When we get our hands on dat, we can shut dis bitch down and do what we gotta do. They probably ain't worrying about nobody over here in Compton even trying them. Those be the sweetest ma'fuckas to hit," Pooty assured him.

Figgady rubbed the hair on his chin and flipped his long dreadlocks over his shoulders. "Nigga, dat's what it is den. What time you tryna kick dis shit off?"

"Tonight. We gon' catch they ass about three in the morning. That's the time where most ma'fuckas in Los Angeles either sleeping, fucking, or laid up wit' a bitch. I already got two of my block hoes kicking it wit' dem niggas right now feeding me everything that's going on. So before sun up, our bag gon' be all the way up. Know dat."

Figgady took a seat at the table. "Say, potna, a ma'fucka wanna thank you on some real shit for letting me roll out here. I know I'm intruding on your life and shit. I just wanna let you know that it's love though."

Pooty waved him off. "It's good, nigga. I wasn't on shit. It was boring as a ma'fucka before you came. We only got a li'l bit of family out here, and the ones that we do have, I ain't dat close to them. It's just feel good to have some family here that I really fuck wit'."

Linda stepped into the kitchen wearing a short robe that clung to her curves. She was light-skinned, mixed Black and Mexican. She rocked a short hairstyle that complemented her pretty face. She stepped up to Pooty and kissed his lips. In order to do so, she had to step onto her tippy toes. Pooty grabbed her fat ass and massaged the cheeks. "Good morning, baby."

"Good morning," he returned, all over her booty.

When he took his hands away, Figgady saw how the robe rested on the top of her chubby ass cheeks before she fixed it. Linda was 5'2" tall and weighed 127 pounds and the majority of her weight was in her ass. Figgady had to look away. He didn't want to be lusting after his cousin's woman.

Linda stepped to the refrigerator and popped back on her legs. "What's on y'all agenda for today?" She grabbed the leftover platter of ribs out of the refrigerator and set it on the countertop.

"We plotting, shorty. Ma'fuckas gotta get their bread all the way up. I been wanting to buss a few moves, but I ain't have the right niggas around me. Now dat my cousin in town, I wanna make his visit count."

Linda slipped four big pieces of rib onto her plate. "You finna make a difference in Los Angeles, Figgady?"

"You muthafuckin' right. Dat's why I'm here," he said, looking her over. She was so bad to him. She reminded him of a finer version of Chela. Chela was his baby mother.

She laughed. "Well, don't let my man get you into trouble. It's a lot of positive things that take place in Los Angeles that you can get into. It ain't all gotta be negative." She smiled at him and placed her food in the microwave. The scent of her perfume lit up the kitchen.

Pooty walked over to her and wrapped his fingers into her hair nicely as if he was playing with her silky strands, then he tightened his grip and yanked her hair so hard that a few strands ripped out of her scalp. He grabbed her by throat and slammed her into the refrigerator. The loaves of bread and cereal that were on top of it fell to the floor. He squeezed and applied a lot of pressure. "Bitch, what I tell you."

She slapped at his hand. Her eyes bugged out of her head. She couldn't breathe. She couldn't swallow. She felt like she was about to be killed. She knew that Pooty was a lunatic. She never knew when he would snap out an actually kill her.

"Bitch, what I tell you!" he growled, still choking.

Linda swiped her hand and opened the refrigerator on accident. The light popped on. She dug her nails into Pooty's side. She began to get lightheaded.

Pooty slid his face next to hers. "Bitch, my niggas is my niggas. My bidness is my bidness. You don't talk to, nor do you flirt wit', my niggas. Dat shit'll get yo' li'l ass snuffed.

You understand that?" He pushed her to the ground. He turned on the sink and used the sprayer to wet her up.

Linda struggled to breathe. She coughed on the floor, lying on her back while Pooty wet her up. She had her thighs splayed wide open. Figgady could see directly between them. She was without underwear. Her pussy lips were chunky. He could see a hint of her inner lips.

Linda scooted backward on the ground. "You said yo' niggas, Pooty. You said only yo' guys. Dat's yo' ma'fuckin' cousin!" she screamed. She used the sink to help her get to her feet. She coughed and spit in it before turning around to face them. Her whole robe was basically transparent. Her big areoles were visible.

Pooty grabbed the food out of the microwave. "Bitch, take dis shit upstairs and eat. Don't bring yo' monkey ass back downstairs while I'm conducting bidness, you got that?"

She grabbed the food from him and stood there mugging him for a moment. Her hair had become wavy. Her sideburns curled up slightly. "You ain't have to do me like that, Pooty. Damn, you ain't have to embarrass me in front of yo' peoples like dat." She walked off into the living room, mumbling to herself.

Pooty took a mop and began to clean up his mess. "Bitch be getting on my nerves sometimes. Only reason I stay wit' her ass is because she held me down while I was in San Quintin."

Figgady shook his head. "Nigga, you my cousin, and I love you to death. On some real shit doe, you just treated the fuck outta shawty for no reason. On me, you snapped. My word, cuz."

Pooty waved him off. "Nigga, dis Cali, this is how we treat bitches out dis way. You gon' find dat out real quick. Now

come downstairs so we can get dis mission in order. We on dis shit tonight."

Figgady grabbed his glass of Mollie and followed him into the basement. "A'ight, but I still stand by what I said."

Miguelito dropped the last eighth of crystal into the mini Ziploc bag and sealed it tight. He stood up from the table and stretched his arms over his head. He felt drowsy. He needed to get back over to Oakland where he could rest peacefully. He didn't trust Compton. There were too many rival gangs, and way too much anarchy for him. He chose to stay where he had control of things. With Mudman holding it down for the Black side of the narcotics world in Oakland, and him conquering the rest of the Game, he felt that he was in the best possible position to take over a cartel back in his native land of Sinaloa. The Bull gave him room to blossom. He knew that. Now all he had to do was to make a lot of money real fast and he would be promoted. He adjusted his gun on his waist. "Say, everything is finally bagged and tagged. The number is two hundred and fifty thousand dollars. You got six days to make this happen," he said this to the table of young hungry Mexicans that depended on the narcotics world in order to feed their families. Most were fighting to secure a slot so they could bring their families over from Mexico. Others were slaves of the Bull's cartel. They were forced to work under Miguelito. It was either that, or to die a torturous death. "Do you vatos hear me?" he asked all of them.

They nodded their heads.

"Awright then. I'll be in touch throughout." He gave the signal, and two of the young shooters followed him to the door and out to his Benz. Once inside he pulled off into the night, headed back to Oakland.

Figgady loafed in the neighbor's yard. He placed the binoculars to his eyes and watched as the Mexicans made their way back to the alley. They stared until the Benz left the alley and turned onto the street. As soon as it did, the Mexicans shook up and patted each other on the back. They stopped to pull out cigarettes, one lighting the other's for him. Then they proceeded to smoke.

Figgady smiled under his Obama mask. He placed the binoculars into his inside coat pocket and cocked the Tech .9. When he looked up, Pooty was already jumping the fence.

Pooty landed in the grass. He kept low and ran up behind the first young Mexican. He grabbed his around the forehead with his arm and sliced his throat. Before the other one could react, he placed his silenced .40 Glock to his Adam's apple and pulled the trigger twice, knocking big holes inside of his throat. He was dead before he hit the ground beside his buddy. Pooty took off running toward the entrance to the trap.

Figgady looked on, amazed. He hopped the fence and hurried inside behind his cousin. When he got inside, he saw his cousin going on a rampage. He finger fucked his Glock and spilled blood all over the living room. Figgady jumped right on bidness. He rushed through the house. When he got to the kitchen, he saw two dope boys trying to run out of the back door. Each had a duffle bag in his hand. Figgady ran a little bit, and then stopped. He extended his arm and squeezed the trigger of his Tech.

The dope boys shook on their feet. The bullets entered into their backs and chopped them down. Figgady rushed over and yanked the bags away from them. He knelt down and looked inside of them. When he saw all of the Ziploc bags of crystal

meth, his eyes lit up. "Hell yeah. Now we talking." He kicked them into the pantry and got back to work. He ransacked the house beside his cousin.

They found three thousand dollars in cash and three liters of PCP. They fucked up the trap so bad that it looked like the Feds had run through it.

"A'ight, let's get the fuck up out of here!" Pooty yelled.

Figgady didn't put up a fight. He stepped over body after body. He made it back to the pantry and grabbed the two bags of crystal. He threw one to Pooty before they rushed back into the night.

"Nigga, where the fuck did you learn all dat weird-ass shit you was doing back there?" Figgady asked as they broke their spoils down the middle.

Pooty nodded in and out. He scratched at his arm. "The army. You know I did a tour of duty before I went to prison, didn't you?"

Figgady shook his head. "Nigga, nall, ain't nobody tell me dat."

"Yep." Pooty nodded out again. "Nigga, ask my mama if you don't believe me." He closed his eyes.

Shid, I believe you. After what I just saw, you gotta be telling the truth. We finna set this city on fire."

Pooty laughed and closed his eyes tighter. He fell back and allowed for the Tar to take over his body. "You damn right we is. Dem niggas out in Oakland don't even know what's about to hit dem."

Figgady laughed. "And dat's the best part about all dis shit. Murder mo', murder mo'." He laughed before his eyes turned into angry balls of fire.

Hood Rich

Chapter 5

"Baby, dis nigga got me all off my square. I feel like every-where I look, I'm seeing him. I can't focus. I can't concen-trate. I can't believe he still alive," Keisha said as she pushed her Jaguar truck. It was black on black, with the all-pink inte-rior. She had her name stitched in the headrests. Whenever things got tough, all she had to do was to hop inside of the truck and cruise. The cruising had a way of helping her ease her anxieties.

Mudman scanned the sunny streets for any sight of attack-ers, jack boys, or even Twelve. He glanced into his rearview mirror to make sure they were being tailed by his security de-tail. After confirming that they were, he breathed easily. The attack on Miguelito's trap house out in Compton had him a bit rattled. Then there were two of his that had been hit in a span of twenty four hours. He'd lost a total of seven hundred thou-sand dollars. Four hundred thousand of it had belonged to The Bull. The Bull was head of The Blood Thirsty Cartel back in Sinaloa, Mexico. Mudman was a bit rattled because the jack boys hadn't left alive a soul inside of the trap house. Mudman knew that was how killas from Baton Rouge got down. His mind had been stuck in wonderment on the thought of the jack boys having something to do with Prentice. If that was the case, he knew he was in for a rude awakening.

"Baby, did you hear what I said?" Keisha asked. She was starting to panic. She drove alongside the coast of Malibu. Something about the scenery was calming to her. One day she hoped that they would be able to own property out that way.

"I heard you, shawty. You need to chill though. You giv-ing dat nigga way too much energy. If dat ma'fucka loafing around Oakland somewhere, we gon' find his ass. You gotta

thank about it. He took a lot of slugs, so he can't be as strong as you giving him credit for."

"Dat nigga ain't gotta be strong. He know how to shoot just fine. On top of dat, he ain't come alone. He had some other niggas wit' him. They had sticks and were blowing at me too." Keisha referred to Prentice's niggas' guns as sticks, just as most people out in Oakland called guns.

That revelation made Mudman slightly nervous. He wondered who the hell Prentice had gotten to roll to with him from Baton Rouge. "Even still, shawty. Dat nigga ain't gon' be here long before I catch him, and when I do, it's gon' be over wit'. Dis time I'ma hit his ass wit' all face shots. Ain't no getting up from dat. Trust me when I tell you dat."

Keisha shook her head. She ran her fingers through her hair and looked over to Mudman, worried. "You know the police been sweating me to talk about the night that Sandra was killed. They keep asking me a million questions. I can't keep running back and forth to that station, Rome. Dat shit driving me crazy."

Mudman handed her two pink Mollie pills. "Shawty, pop dis shit 'cause you doing way too much ma'fuckin' stressing. I ain't never seen you dis rattled. You giving dat nigga way too much ma'fuckin' energy."

Keisha popped the pills and chased them with a Vitamin Water. "I don't know why the fuck you so calm. Just like he want me dead, he want yo' ass dead too. You should be just as worried." She continued driving.

Mudman sat in silence for a moment, playing back what she had just said to him. He thought about it until he grew angry. "Wait a minute. Fuck is you saying, Keisha? You thank I'm worried about this lowlife-ass nigga? Huh?"

"Mudman, I ain't saying it like that. I'm just saying - " Keisha started.

"Fuck Prentice and all dem niggas back home. They don't wanna see me," he snapped. He picked the Draco up from the side of the door and set it on to his lap. "Dat nigga Prentice want this smoke, den he can get it. Dis time I'ma empty the whole clip in his ass, and dis bitch shoot a hunnit rounds. I plan on winning every round I buck, 'cause I'ma make dese bitches count," he spat. "You should already know how I get down, bitch."

Keisha mugged him and kept rolling. "Nigga, calm yo' crazy ass down. Ain't nobody saying dat you can't handle dis nigga. I'm just saying that you should have a little more concern than you seem to have. We don't know where he coming from, who he coming with, and most importantly, when he coming. All we know is that he out there, and dat nigga is scorned."

Mudman grunted and wiped his nose. "Like I said before, fuck dat nigga. Whenever he pop up, I'ma be ready. Ain't no nigga finna have me spooked. I ain't afraid to take my slab in the morgue. It is what it is."

Keisha swallowed her spit. "Yeah, well, all dat shit sound good, but I ain't ready to die just yet. I'm still young, and I got a whole lot more living to do. We just starting to see bundles of cash. I wanna travel. I wanna live good. I wanna hit yo' pockets a lot," she joked seriously.

Mudman nodded. "I already know yo' ass do. You da only ma'fucka that can hit my pockets. The safe closed to anybody else, but you earned that right."

"You muthafuckin' right I did. I caught more than a few slugs fuckin' wit' you. That's why I'm saying I'm too young to die. We need to find his ass and slay him. It's as simple as that."

"Yeah, well, I'm working on it. I put fifty G's up, and I'm praying I can make back the four hundred thousand that we

lost for The Bull, or else we gon' have a whole other mutha-fucka to worry about that's deadlier than Prentice." Mudman shook his head. "I need to mellow out. Let's roll back to da crib so I can get my system right. The sooner I do that, the better."

"Mudman, can I tell you something without you getting angry?" Keisha asked, constantly glancing at him from the corners of her eyes.

Mudman was starting to feel his sick come on. He needed to get the Sinaloa Tar up his nostrils, and quick. He felt like his stomach was turning into a knot. "You can tell me any-thang long as you keep this truck rolling toward the house."

"I'm three months pregnant." She kept rolling, refusing to look over at him now.

"Why you just telling me dis now?"

She shrugged her shoulders. "I wasn't gon' say shit period until we got past that danger zone. You remember all dat shit the doctors were saying about me going to have issues with conceiving, and carrying the baby its full term because of the bullet wounds, right?"

He nodded. "Yeah."

"Well, I was just a li'l worried about getting your hopes all up high. I couldn't devastate you like dat again. I don't think I could watch the expression on your face knowing that I had failed you for a second time. I just couldn't."

"Shawty, what you talking 'bout? You ain't fail me the first time. Dat nigga deliberately shot you in your stomach to kill our baby. Dat's how dat happened. It ain't shit to do wit' you failing me."

"I know, but still. The only time I ever saw you smile for more than a few seconds was when we were talking about how the baby was going to be. Or when you laid your face on my

stomach so you could talk to it. You gotta admit that you were just as excited as I was."

Mudman nodded. "I was. Just keeping that shit a hunnit. But it's all good. Dat's what happens when you in a war. Casualties take place. In dis case, we lost our baby. But it seems like God put another one in hurr, huh?" He reached across the console and rubbed her stomach through her Fendi dress.

"Yeah, baby. Lord willing, dis one be able to make it to full term." Keisha was nervous. She had very little faith that something serious was not about to happen to the both of them. She knew how the Game went. You lived by the sword, and ultimately you would die by it. She had taken more than her few shares of lives. It was only a matter of time before the same things happened to both her and Mudman, she felt.

Mudman rubbed her stomach more firmly. "I'ma make sure of dat." He grew angry at the thought of something happening to Keisha or their child. "Matter fact, until I find Prentice, you getting the fuck out of Oakland. I'm sending yo' ass to Los Angeles to lay low."

"Los Angeles? Who the fuck we know in Los Angeles?" she questioned.

"Don't worry about it. Dat's where you finna go soon as I set it up. You want me to start to take dis nigga more seriously, den dat's what I'm finna do. When you get back to the crib, pack yo' shit, and we gon' go from dere."

Keisha frowned. "You so fuckin' controlling. You lucky I love yo; crazy ass, or else I'd tell you to kiss my ass."

"Shawty, I'd kiss dat ma'fucka and still make yo' ass get up out of dis war zone," Mudman said, laying back. "Dat's what real love do. Case closed."

Figgady started to feel sick to his stomach. The mini yacht floated up and down on the water. He was started to get seasick. He clutched his stomach and leaned into Pooty's ear. "Say, mane, when we gon' make dis move? I'm starting to feel sick as hell."

Pooty eyed his mark through his Gucci shades. He adjusted them on his nose. His heart beat faster and faster. "Nigga, I told you to drank some of dat Syrup before you came on dis lick. Dis ma'fucka got dese goods, and I ain't leaving off of dis boat until we get what I came for." He walked away from Figgady and toward the front of the boat.

Figgady stood against the railing. He took a deep breath and felt his stomach turn upside down. His insides seemed to drop all the way down to the lower pits of his stomach, and then he was throwing up into the Pacific Ocean with his eyes closed tightly.

Ralph laughed and slid his arm around Pooty's shoulder. He was 5'7" tall and Italian. He owned a bunch of property in Pooty's hood and was his current landlord, amongst other things. "Yo' cousin. He don't get off of land very much, I take it?" Ralph asked.

Pooty shook his head. "He a country boy. Ain't nothing but swamps and shit where he stay."

"That's a shame. Everybody should get a chance to enjoy these sights." He slid his arm from around Pooty's shoulders and walked to the deck of the boat with his binoculars. He placed them to his eyes and caught sight of the boat he was looking for. His supplier told him that they would have an orange flag waving in the front of their boat. That would be his signal to know that it was them. "About time. Here they are."

Pooty took the binoculars from him and saw the boat. He smiled and tried to calm himself. Ralph had hired him as security for the pick-up as he had done on many missions so

many times before. Pooty had displayed his loyalty as he watched the older man pull in pounds after pounds of crystal. His greed had finally gotten the better of him. Ralph was set to pull in a half million dollars of product, and Pooty had to have it. He was coming for the slums of Compton. He was dying to conquer the deadly streets that had raised him. He had so many people depending on him to pull off the caper that he refused to lose. "A'ight, so what you want me to do?"

"It's quite simple, really. They are going to pull their boat closer to ours. We'll toss over the duffel bag of money. They'll go through it briefly, and then toss over my product. I don't need to check it. The Sinaloas don't play about their shit. Once we get the shipment on this boat, we're free to leave. The reason you're here is just like other times. I need you to watch my back. Just in case things don't go as planned. I don't know why they wouldn't, but you know what kind of field were dabbling in. The only ma'fucka I trust is you."

"And vice versa," Pooty lied. "A'ight, I got you."

Figgady came over, wiping his mouth. "What's good?"

"The shipment coming in right there. We gotta get on security," Pooty relayed.

Figgady looked into the distance and saw the boat. "Aw shit, a'ight, cool." He took out his pistol and ducked into the cabin of the boat.

Five minutes later, Pooty grunted while he pulled the shipment of meth into the boat. He knelt down and unzipped it for Ralph to look inside of it. Ralph saw the numbered packages. The Cartel always numbered their packages so they could know what amount was going where, and what was supposed to be their intake from them.

"Looks good to me! Tell The Bull I'll have his cash for this in three weeks!" he hollered at the messenger for The Bull.

The masked Mexican nodded. He waved his hand. His boat lurched forward. Then he and his two security men were driving away with their engine revving as it spit water behind them.

Ralph stood up and dusted off his hands. "Well, that's just that. Easy as one, two, three," he said, looking down at the work. When he finally looked up, he was staring into the cold, black face of Pooty. A chill went through him. "Pooty, what's the matter? What is it?"

Figgady stepped in back of him and placed the barrel of his .45 to his head. He waited for Pooty to step to the side before he pulled the trigger twice, splattering the deck with Ralph's brains. He stood over him and gave him two face shots.

Pooty dragged him to the railing of the boat, picked him up, and threw him over. Then he let down the spare boat that was on the side of the mini yacht. He loaded in the duffel bag before he and Figgady roared away, talking about how Ralph's body floated for a few seconds before it sank into the ocean.

Chapter 6

Mudman knocked twice on Ashley's door. He looked both ways in the hallway and adjusted the .40 Glock in his waistband. At the end of the hallway on each side, he had security placed. Though he was the supreme leader of the Acorn Projects, he knew that he could never be too careful.

Ashley looked through the peep hole and stood back. She smiled, knowing that Mudman was standing outside of her door. She pulled her long hair out of its bun and allowed for it to fall down her back. She ran her fingers through it and fixed her bra so that her golden melons were on display. Then she opened the door.

The first thing Mudman smelled was her perfume and the scent of shampoo coming from her hair. He looked her up and down. She wore a pair of tight booty shorts that exposed her thick thighs under a cut-off white beater. Her long hair fell over her shoulders and hung around her waist. He stepped inside and closed the door. "What's good, li'l mama?"

She slid into his arms and hugged him. "Hey daddy. I was hoping you was gon' show up." She took a step back and kissed him on the cheek.

Mudman rubbed all over her ass, squeezing the cheeks. "You already know that whenever you need me, I'm coming." He leaned down his head and kissed her on the forehead.

Ashley smiled and hugged him tighter. "You hungry?" She walked away with her shorts all inside of her yellow ass cheeks. When she took a step with her right foot, it caused that side's cheek to jiggle, and it did the same with the left. Mudman couldn't help enjoying the view of her. He found her so sexy.

"Nall, I'm good. Tell me what's going on?" He locked the door and eased into the living room. He took a seat, placing his pistol on his lap.

Ashley poured him a glass of orange juice and brought it to him. She personally didn't like the taste of it. She had bought an entire jug for him. It was the only thing she could get him to consume when he came over. "There's really no problem, Mudman, I just wanted to spend some time with you. I know I can't act on how I really feel around other people, and I guess it's just starting to take a wear and tear on me a li'l bit. I'm crazy about you, and I need more of you." She eased into his lap and sat down. Her right arm went around his shoulder. She looked into his eyes with her green ones.

Mudman held her and took a sip from the juice. "What I tell you about catching all dem feelings and shit, huh?"

She lowered her head. "You told me not to do it. But I can't help it, Mudman. I ain't like dese other hoes out there. I can't detach myself from you after we've been intimate. I wish I could, but I just can't. Being around you drives me crazy. I don't be knowing what to do with myself. I'm just being honest." She slid her face into his neck and sucked along it, gradually adding teeth. Her left leg swung across his waist until she was straddling him on the couch.

Mudman laid back his head. Tingles shot through his body as Ashley did her thing. He felt himself getting hard right away. It was always like that whenever he was in her presence. "Bitch, but I told you what it is. Didn't I?"

"Yes, daddy, you did. I just can't help it."

More sucking. More kissing. The feeling kept getting better and better for Mudman. He rose, and picked her up. She continued to kiss all over his neck while he carried her. When he got to the bedroom, he dropped her on the bed and took off his shirt, revealing his ripped chocolate body.

Ashley felt her pussy purr. She sucked her bottom lip and rubbed the crease of her shorts. She was without panties. "I want you, daddy. Please gimme some of you."

"Bitch, you hard headed. Get yo' ass on yo' elbows and knees," Mudman ordered. He stripped down.

Ashley followed his commands. She pointed her big ass toward him and pulled her shorts upward so that they were in her crack. Mudman saw the mold of her cat. It was damp. The lips were easily visible. "Touch me, daddy. Please."

Mudman grabbed her waist and pulled her over his lap. He positioned her just perfectly, rubbing all over her ass. "You feeling some type of way about me, huh?" His fingers dipped into her crease. They played over her lips.

"Yes, daddy. I can't help it," she whispered.

"But what I tell you to do? No what?" He slammed his hand down on her ass hard. Smack!

"Feelings!" Ashley hollered. She ground her front into his lap. "Please touch me!" she gritted through her teeth.

Mudman held her waist more firmly. He raised his hand in the air. "You don't run shit. I do. You run under me. Don't you understand dat shit?" Smack! Smack! Smack! Smack! He proceeded to smack her ass cheeks with no mercy. First the right one. Then the left. Then he smacked the middle, and followed the same pattern again. He watched them jiggle and shake.

"Oh! Oh! Dad-deee! Shit! It hurts!" She ground harder into his lap. She could feel herself oozing.

Mudman yanked the shorts upward harder. Now both of her sex lips were exposed. They were golden red and naked. He played over them with his finger before locating her clitoris through the material of her shorts. He pinched it.

"Uhhhh!" Ashley ground her pelvis as hard as she could into his lap and came. She shivered, digging her nails into his thigh.

Mudman pushed her off of his lap and onto her stomach. He climbed behind her before stuffing his face into her gap from the back. He yanked her shorts to the side. Her pussy popped out, engorged. He sucked it into his mouth and began to perform magic.

Ashley clutched the bedsheets and screamed into the pillow. It felt like Mudman was exploring parts of her pussy that she didn't even know she had. He worked miracles on her clit with his tongue. He sucked it through his gap and drove her crazy.

Ashley smushed her ass all into his face. She wagged it from side to side. She held her cheeks open to give him greater access to her treasures. Her eyes continued to roll into the back of her head. She shivered and came a second time when his tongue entered deep into her sex. She screamed into the pillow and fell on her stomach.

Mudman yanked her shorts off and tossed them to the floor. "You wanna take my bitch's place, don't you?" he asked, pumping his piece.

Ashley laid on her back, rubbing her pussy as she watched him. Her clit was still highly sensitive from her double climaxes. She shook her head from right to left. "I just wanna play my role to the tee. Whatever position you gon' give me, I'ma master dat shit, daddy. Long as you give me some time with you." She slipped her middle finger into herself.

Mudman stroked his piece faster. "Come over here and suck dis ma'fucka. Make me proud. Hurry up."

Ashley hurried across the bed. She took ahold of held piece and flipped her long hair over her shoulders. She licked her lips and sucked him into her mouth, going to work.

Mudman worked his hips. He tried to avoid looking into her green eyes. It was a trigger for him. In his opinion, she was too fine for her own good. That's why he felt he needed to treat her like he did. He couldn't take it easy on her. He grabbed a handful of her hair and fucked her face at full speed. She arched her back and spaced her thighs. He squeezed her ass and rubbed into her crack, fingering her faster and faster.

Ashley pumped her fist as fast as she could. She sucked harder. She felt his piece jerk twice. He stuffed it further into her mouth and came back to back. She continued to pump and stroke him. His seed tasted like victory to her. She felt that it made her stronger. It brought her closer to him.

Mudman cringed as she licked around his head and lightly nipped at it with her teeth, just enough to buckle him. He pushed her away and walked to her dresser. He opened the top drawer and grabbed a wet wipe, cleansing himself.

Ashley climbed to her knees. "Daddy, please tell me we ain't done," she whined.

"Shawty, stop playin' wit' me. You already know what dis is."

She felt defeated. "But I need you. I ain't had none in a long time. I'm feening for you. Please, just put it in."

Mudman grabbed his boxers off of the floor. "Only bitch that earned dis dick is Keisha. You ain't paid enough dues to get none of dis pipe, li'l girl."

Ashley slid out of the bed. She stood before him, bad. Her body was flawless. Both of her nipples were erect and protruding from her mounds. She rubbed her cat. By this time, it was leaking. "You ain't finna do me like dis. You finna have to whoop my ass 'cause you finna give me some of dat dick, daddy." She was trying to muster up the courage to go at him. She balled up her fists.

Mudman laughed. "Shawty, shut yo' ass up and go get in the shower."

She shook her head. "Nope. Gimme some of dat pipe. Now!" More of her juices ran down her inner thighs. She took a step forward.

Mudman stood watching her with his pipe hanging low. He tried his best to keep from laughing. He was trying to really figure out if she was serious. Though they had played around a few times, it had never progressed past oral sex. He'd never fucked a female behind Keisha's back. He felt that it would have been disloyal of him to do so, but Ashley was making it hard on him. "Shawty, go do like I said."

"You heard me. Ain't!" she snapped.

He grabbed her by the throat. "Bitch!"

She grabbed his piece and squeezed it. "Fuck me," she croaked.

He let her go. "I already told you what dis was. Keep playin', and I'ma replace yo' ass."

Ashley wasn't trying to hear none of what he was talking about. Her pussy was jumping on the inside. She needed him. She jumped on him and wrapped her thighs around his body. His hard piece lined up with her slippery crease. She reached between them and inserted the head into her slit before pushing down on it. "Unnnnnn!"

Mudman closed his eyes. His knees became wobbly. He fell to the bed with ten inches deep. Before he could think about the betrayal, he was pounding her out as hard as he could. The headboard beat against the wall with a steady tap tap tap tap.

Ashley moaned louder and louder. Mudman dug her out. He was fucking her so hard and fast that she felt like she couldn't breathe. She couldn't believe that he was inside of her. The deeper he traveled, the more she wanted.

Mudman flipped her on her side and yanked her to him. He stood on the side of the bed, nailing her. She looked so good, he thought. Her sex faces had him ready to blow. "Bitch. Whose. Pussy. Is. Dis?" He tossed her right ankle over his shoulder, fucking her with brute intensity.

Ashley's mouth was wide open. Drool slipped out of it and wet her cheek. Her eyelids fluttered. "Yours. Yours. Dadeeeee!" She screamed, cumming. Tears seeped out of her eyes. The dick was whipping her. She had never gotten it like Mudman was giving it to her. She felt like she was in sexual heaven. "Yours!"

Mudman clenched his teeth and went as fast and as hard as he could. He dug his fingers into her flesh and continued to yank her back to him over and over again. He felt her insides suck at him. Then he was cumming hard. "Arrgh! Fuck!" he groaned. Ashley screamed that she was cumming at the same time his seed spilled from him into her womb. He yanked it out and came in squirts all over her belly.

Ashley felt the hot jets, and shivered on the bed. Her Kitty's mouth was wide open, and leaking. She opened the lips further and ran her middle finger in circles around her clit as he filled her skin with his semen.

Two hours later, after their shower, she lay on top of him, playing with his earlobe. Her face rested in the crux of his neck.

"I can't help how much I love you, Mudman. It don't matter what happens in those streets, or what we go through as a cartel, you da the only nigga that can do me like you do. If you hate me for dat, then it's cool. Maybe I got a lot to learn. I mean, I'm only eighteen," Ashley whispered to him.

Mudman gripped that fat ass. He massaged the cheeks. She felt so hot on top of him. Hot, but good. He was feeling some type of way because he had fucked another female without Keisha knowing, but he reasoned with himself that he would tell her what was good later. To him, Ashley really wasn't that big of a deal. She was simply young pussy. All of the bosses in the game had a young duck off. He was thinking that she could be his.

"Shawty, you can't control how you feel. You a'ight. Just don't bring dem emotions into the field. Shut dat shit off when I climb out of dis bed. Dat's an order. You hear me?"

She nodded. "Yeah, I'll try." She kissed his cheek and rubbed it while her green eyes searched over his face in the moonlight. "You think Keisha gon' hate me when she find out about what we did?"

Mudman shrugged his shoulders. "Probably. She already don't trust yo' li'l yellow ass. She always talking 'bout how pretty you is." He laughed.

"Yeah, well, make sure she know that I'm cool wit' being the side bitch. Like Moneybagg said, sometimes side bitches be more than the main hoes do. I'm not saying she a hoe or nothin' like dat, but you get my drift." She rested her head on his chest. "Damn, you got me nuts though. I think I should have never allowed for you to put your piece in me." She kissed his chest.

Mudman kissed the top of her head. "It's all good, li'l mama. I got'chu. Just keep doing da shit you been doing, and you ain't gotta worry about nothin'. I put three bands in dat top drawer over dere to help you wit' dem bills. I know shit get hard. Dat's why I'm hurr doe."

Ashley rubbed all over his abs. She loved the way the muscles looked inside of the chocolate skin. "Mudman, can I tell you something?"

"Go 'head, shawty."

"Before you came out here to Cokeland, dis bitch was full of suckas. Dese niggas wasn't hitting on nothin'. Now that you got this ma'fucka locked down, you got everybody stepping up their killa. I love you for dat. I mean, I know I tell you dat I love you a lot. It's just 'cause I do. I appreciate you." She slid beside him and tossed her thigh over his waist.

Mudman held her more firmly in his arms. "Like I said, I got chu."

"I know you do."

Bomp! Bomp! Bomp! Bomp! Came a beating on Ashley's door.

Mudman jumped up and slipped into his clothes without his boxers quickly. He grabbed his gun. "Shawty, stay yo' ass in hurr."

Ashley already had her .9 millimeter in her hand. "You got me fucked up. Daddy, I'm riding beside you." She slid a long T-shirt over her head.

Mudman rushed to the front door. "Mane, who da fuck is it?"

"Mars, boss. We got a situation over at the City Towers."

Mudman opened the door. "What happened?"

"I'll explain everything to you on the way. I thank..." Mars stopped when he saw Ashley in the state of undress that she was in. He, unbeknownst to her or Mudman, still had feelings for her. He frowned. "What, y'all fuckin' now?"

"Nigga, fall back. I'll be out in a minute." Mudman closed the door in his face. He turned to Ashley and snatched her up, sucking all over her neck, palming that fat ass. "Shawty, I'ma get up with you later on. Hold ya head, a'ight?"

She nodded. "Yes, daddy. I'm back in the field tomorrow."

"You damn right. Remember, leave dem feelings in dat bedroom. I need killa shit in you at all times. Me coming hurr is yo' reward. Feel dat?"

Ashley smiled and stepped on her tippy toes, wrapping her arms around his neck. "Yes daddy."

Chapter 7

Mudman sat in the passenger seat of Mars's Lexus truck, feeling uncomfortable. He'd fucked up and left his boxers back at Ashley's apartment, and now he could feel his piece running against the material of his jeans. "Explain to me what happened?"

"All dey telling me is dat ma'fuckas ransacked the building. Four of our traps got hit. It's bodies all up and down the hallway, and the police ain't fucking wit' the area at all. That's a good thing though because it gives you time to assess the damage." Mars still couldn't believe that Mudman was fucking Ashley.

"Damn, how da fuck they get past our security?" Mudman asked, irritated.

"Don't know, but they did." He was quiet for a split second. "So you and Ashley fuckin' around now?"

Mudman glared at him. He twisted the cap off of his bottled water that he'd dropped two Mollies inside of. "Nigga, why are you in my muthafuckin' bidness?"

"I'm not, but you know I got a li'l girl by shawty. She out in San Francisco wit' my mama for two weeks. I just wanna know what it is so I can know what kind of environment my daughter gon' be subjected to."

Mudman took a huge swallow from his bottle, so much so that it folded inward. "Nigga, miss me wit' dat nosy shit. Whatever me and shawty wanna do, we gon' do it, and ain't shit you gon' do about it. Yo' daughter ain't in harm's way if we was to fuck around. She in San Francisco, remember?" Mudman looked him off.

Mars got heated quickly. He hated how Mudman spoke to him as if he was a bitch. He wanted to say something to that effect, but he figured that it could only lead down the wrong

path. "I thought you and Keisha was one hunnit doe. Why you fuckin' on Ashley all of da sudden?"

Mudman mugged him. "Nigga, why da fuck you keep asking me about dis bitch? Mind yo' fuckin' bidness. Dat bitch ain't checking for you. Second to dat, me and Keisha one hunnit. Dat's my day one. Get your mind right, li'l one, fo' I buss ya brain. You doing too much. You sounding like a bitch right now. Dat's on da clique." Mudman's heart was pounding in his chest. "Just drive dis ma'fucka truck and get me to my buildings. Simple as dat."

Mars bit his tongue like a sucka. "Yeah, a'ight. I'ma do just dat."

Mudman entered into the first floor hallway twenty minutes later, and he couldn't believe his eyes. As soon as he stepped into the building, there were two dead bodies. Both male, both shooters that worked under him. They had blood oozing out of wounds in their heads. He stepped over them and continued down the hallway. The first floor was where he sold his pure powder coke and rock. He walked past three apartment doors that were opened. His workers stood in the doorways with worried expressions on their faces. The looks angered him. It made him feel like a failure. As he continued down the hallway, he came to another door. He stepped inside of the apartment that he used for a cooking house. He saw three bodies in the living room. All three were naked females. All three had been murdered execution style. Inside of the kitchen were two more women. They lay face down in a puddle of blood. Bullets had been fired to the back of their heads. He shook his own head. He looked around. The table where

they chopped their dope up had been flipped over. Powder residue was all over the carpet. The carpet was soggy with blood. Earlier that day, Mudman had dropped off four kilos of coke. He valued each brick at fifty thousand. That was two hundred thousand that he would lose. Two hundred thousand that belonged to The Bull. He cursed under his breath.

Mars came into the room and looked around. "Damn, who da fuck would kill all of dese innocent bitches?" he asked.

Mudman ignored him. Prentice came to his mind right away. He knew his M.O. When it came down to hitting a lick, they killed the entire trap. That's how Baton Rouge had bred them. Mudman felt like Prentice was hunting him. He shook his head again and stepped back into the hallway. After only a few short steps, he ran across two more bodies. Both male. Thy looked as if they had been chopped down by an assault rifle to him. Mudman grew angrier. After going over the entire building he counted ten dudes and six females that he'd lost for workers. The jack boys had gotten away with a total of six kilos of coke and twenty thousand in cash. That was three hundred and twenty thousand in cash all together. There was no way that Mudman could take the loss lying down. He already had to answer for the losses that he'd taken only a week prior. The Bull had made it perfectly clear that he didn't honor excuses. He'd either get his bread, or he made you pay in blood. That's how he handled business.

It took Mudman all of an hour before he came out of the building and huddled up with his group of savages. He stood in the middle while they gathered around him. "Check dis out, ma'fuckas done fucked up now. Since jack boys wanna run off in my shit, now we hunting day ass. I want every muthafuckin' jack boy in the city brought to me. I don't give a fuck if you gotta bring dey mama to me first. You bring every one of dem bitches before me so I can get to the bottom of dis. If

I don't get every crumb that was stolen from me today I'm running through households with no mercy. I'm gon' get my shit in blood," he snarled.

Mars nodded his head. "I know just where to start. Assign me three hittas, and we on bidness."

"Pick yo' own men. Matter fact, Mars hurr is head of dis mission. Ma'fuckas do what he say. I need to make some calls." Mudman stepped away from the crowd as they huddled up and discussed how they were about to hunt jack boys. He pulled put his cell phone and called Miguelito, telling him that they needed to sit down and talk ASAP.

Figgady licked his lips and eyed Linda's younger sister Lainey closely. She wore a pair of yoga pants that cuffed her young ass. She was caramel, and so strapped that Figgady couldn't believe it. She wasn't all that pretty to him, but she had him feeling some type of way.

Lainey grabbed a bottle water out of the refrigerator and popped back on her legs. Her ass jiggled in the yoga pants.

She turned around to face Figgady. She smiled. "You been giving me dis crazy look da last few days. What's up wit' you?" she asked, stepping closer to the table that he was sitting at.

Figgady smirked. "Shawty, how old is yo' li'l ass?"

"Old enough to know that you been peeping me real close. You see somethin' you like or what?" Lainey asked. She set down the bottled water. Her breasts jutted up against her tight T-shirt.

Figgady looked both ways. "Where my cousin and yo' sister go?"

62

"Grocery shopping. Why you asking all that when you ain't even answered my question yet?" She came around and stood in front of him. "You see somethin' you like?"

Figgady grabbed her to him. She yelped and wound up with her breasts next to his face. "I asked you how old you is?" He gripped her ass and squeezed the soft cheeks.

"Dat ain't yo' bidness. You low key don't care anyway." She stepped forward. "Do you?"

Figgady really didn't. He knew she had to be young because she was still in school. But he didn't give no fucks. She was too thick for him to truly care. He pulled her closer and kissed her neck. "Li'l girl, I'll wear dis li'l coochie out. Believe dat." He slid his hand into her crease from the back. He felt her hot box. His fingers brushed over the lips.

Lainey moaned. "You ain't gon' do nothin' to me." She pushed him off of her and backed up. She grabbed the bottled water off of the table and headed upstairs with it.

Figgady watched her ascend the steps. Her yoga pants had given her a wedgie. Those cheeks looked righteous to him. She looked back over her shoulder and smiled at him. Figgady jumped out of the chair and turned up his Mollie water. Mollie water was a bottle of water that he'd dropped three capsules of Mollie into. He finished the whole bottle and followed behind Lainey. When he found her standing in the doorway of her bedroom, he stopped in his tracks.

She looked up at him with her brown eyes. "So you following dis jailbait kitty now, huh?"

Figgady walked toward her. When he got close enough, he pulled her to him. He grabbed that ass again. "I don't give a fuck about none of dat. What's really good?"

Lainey tried to push him off. "Get off of me, Figgady. You gon' get me in trouble. Plus I can feel yo' thing poking at me."

Figgady reached under and gripped her fat-ass booty. He held it in his hands while he pounded her out. His lips sucked at her erect nipples. When she screamed into his ear for him to stop a second time, he came, busting back to back.

She pushed him off of her and jumped up. "I'm calling my sister. I'm telling her what you did." She opened the door and ran out of the room.

Figgady jumped from the bed and grabbed his boxers from the floor. He pulled them on and took off after her. "Lainey, come here. Shawty, let me holler at you real quick."

Lainey grabbed her book bag off of the couch and took her cell phone from it. She pulled up Linda's cell phone number and started to dialing.

Figgady ran into the room at full speed and tackled her to the floor. They landed on the coffee table. Lainey was fighting for her life. "Get off of me! Get off of me!" she screamed.

"Shawty, chill. Chill yo' ass out." Figgady grabbed her by the sides of the head and slammed it into the floor as hard as he could, knocking her senseless. Her mouth was wide open with her tongue hanging out of the side of it.

He heard Pooty's truck banging his music loudly. It pulled to the front of the house. He ran to the windows, and peeked out. He saw Linda jump out the truck, followed by Pooty. They popped the back of the truck and began grabbing bags out of it.

Figgady felt like he was about to panic. He rushed back to Lainey's body and dragged her into the guest room that he was staying in on the first floor. He knelt down, and wrapped her neck in his bicep, squeezing as hard as he could. He couldn't stand for her to accuse him of anything. He needed Pooty. He had to get his revenge on Prentice. He had to get Mudman back for snubbing him, snubbing that he felt cost his daughter

her life. He pulled upward and squeezed so hard that he heard her neck snap twice. He kept squeezing for a full minute.

"Figgady! Where you at, cuz?" Pooty hollered.

Figgady jumped up, stuffed Lainey into the closet, and closed the door. "I'm in here getting dressed. I'll be out in a second."

"Good, nigga, we need yo' help wit' these bags," Pooty said, going back outside.

"Lainey, you can bring yo' ass out here and help too," Linda yelled before going back outside.

Figgady opened the closet door one more time. He kicked her body to stuff her further inside. "Stupid ass." He pulled his jacket off of the hanger and covered her with it. "To the river you go." He laughed, closing the door.

Chapter 8

Keisha flipped her curly hair over her shoulders and walked behind Mudman as they overlooked the city of Los Angeles. They were in the Marriott's Presidential Suite, standing on the balcony. It was eight o'clock at night on a hot summer day.

"Baby, I can tell that somethin is wrong wit' you. I thought you'd feel a lot better after looking at the ultrasound pictures of our babies. Is it because I'm holding twins that's stressing you out?" she asked, snuggling up under him.

Mudman stepped out of her embrace, and pulled her into his arms. "Shawty, I'm good. I'm happy that Jehovah is blessing us with two shorties instead of one. It's like he's giving us back the baby that Prentice's bitch ass took from us." He kissed the back of her head.

She smiled and placed her hand on top of his. "Yeah, baby, I think you're right. I can't wait to see what we look like entwined in one body. I know our children are going to be beautiful. I'm still a li'l nervous about carrying them to full term, but I honestly feel like God got a plan for these children. I ain't even been sick like I was with our last baby and I should be, because this time its two babies instead of one. You know?"

Mudman held her closer to him as he looked at the bright lights of the city. From their vantage point, he could see the entire downtown. The city's night life was beautiful to him. "We just gotta take things slow. That's why I need you to chill in dis suite while I get everythang in order."

Keisha turned around to face him. "I'ma do whatever you say, baby. I know you got my best interest at heart." She stepped on her tippy toes and kissed his lips.

Mudman returned her affection. He looked into her pretty brown eyes. "Shawty, I gotta tell you something." He pulled her by the hand back into the hotel room.

"What you gotta tell me?" She was nervous, though she kept a smile on her face.

Mudman led her so that she was sitting on the bed. "Just chill right there." He took a swallow from his bottled water. "A'ight, now don't get to acting all funny and shit. Just know that I wanted to keep shit one hunnit wit you."

"Okay. What is it?" Now she was excited to find out the information. She was trying her best to read Mudman's body language, but as usual, he was giving her nothing.

"I got some pussy a few nights ago."

Keisha popped her head back. "You what?" She stood up.

"Yeah, I was chilling wit' a li'l bitch, and shit just happened. It ain't mean nothing, but I just wanted to put that shit put there to let you know what was good."

Keisha closed the distance between them with blazing speed. She cocked back her hand and slapped him as hard as she could. "What the fuck is wrong wit' you, Mudman! Don't you know I'm pregnant?" she snapped.

Mudman stood there with his face stinging. He flared his nostrils and tried to get ahold of himself. Everything in his head was telling him to fuck Keisha up. But his heart was saying different. His heart told him that Keisha had a right to react how she had. She was the Queen, and though he ran and ruled the streets, when he stepped past their threshold and into her presence, he was supposed to be submissive to his Jewel. "Shawty, dat all you got?" he asked.

Keisha slapped him again and pushed him backward. He only took one step back. She sat on the bed and covered her face. "Mudman, how could you? Since when you start fuckin' random hoes for the sport of it? She must have been too bad to resist, huh?"

Mudman shook his head. His face was stinging. "It wasn't nothing like dat. Shit just happened."

"So it's cool if I take my ass out thurr tonight and fuck some random nigga? Den when you ask me what happened, I'll say da same shit you saying. You gon' be cool wit' dat? Huh?"

"You leave dis room and go fuck wit' any nigga, I'm smoking him, and I'ma beat yo' ass. It's simple as that. You got my seeds inside of you. Ain't no nigga finna be putting his dick in you. Fuck wrong wit'chu?"

She hopped up. "Fuck wrong wit' me? Nigga, what the fuck is wrong wit'chu?" She stepped into his face. "Just like you saying you would have smoked any nigga that I fucked off wit', I wanna smoke da bitch that you screwed. What's fair is fair. Who is the bitch?" Keisha slid her Air Max on and fixed the laces. She grabbed her Birken bag off of the dresser top and dropped her .9 millimeter into it.

Mudman stood there in silence. He knew that if she found out that it was Ashley, she was going to kill her on sight. On the other hand, he couldn't lie to Keisha. Since they had been together, he had never told her a lie. He wasn't about to break that realness just because he'd fucked off for the first time. He was stuck between a rock and a hard place. He cared about Ashley, and he didn't want to see her life taken over one night with him. "Shawty, dat shit ain't even important."

Keisha's eyes shot wide open. "Oh, so you really love this new bitch, huh?" She was taken aback. Not only was she angry, but she felt hurt and betrayed. She felt that Mudman would never do either one to her. She was so hurt that she fighting to stop the tears from coming out of her eyes. Once they started she hated herself. "Who da fuck is she, Mudman? I got a right to know."

Mudman felt sick. He hated when Keisha cried. It always made him feel less than a man. Like he was failing her. Now he was having regrets on ever sleeping with Ashley. "Keisha,

shawty, let's not do dis shit. I just wanted to let you know what took place. Now dat I did, I really need for us to move on. I fucked up, boo." He took a step toward her to embrace her.

Keisha held up both of her hands to stop him. "Nigga, if you don't step yo' monkey ass back, we finna have a big problem."

Mudman stepped back. Now he was getting angry. He hated when she didn't fold when he was ready for her to. "Keisha, so what you finna do, huh? What you wanna do? I told you I fucked. I apologize, baby, damn."

She eyed him angrily from across the room. She slid her hand into her bag and pulled her gun from it. She dropped the bag and held the gun at her side. "Who is dis bitch, Mudman? Give me this hoe's name!" She aimed the gun at him after cocking it. "I swear to God I'll knock yo head off of yo' shoulders if you don't tell me."

Mudman glared at her. "Dat's where you wanna take dis shit? Really?" He stepped in front of her and grabbed the gun. He placed it to his forehead. "A'ight den. Pull dis ma'fucka. Knock my shit off right now, Keisha."

Keisha cocked the hammer. A tear slid out of her right eye and fell down her cheek. She pressed the barrel harder into his dark skinned forehead. "Nigga, what's her fuckin' name? Where can I find dis bitch?"

"Kill me. Fuck you waiting on? You wanna pull dis ma'fucka out. Act like you really 'bout dat life? A'ight, shut the fuck up, and pull the trigger."

Keisha squeezed her eyelids together. She started to imagine life without Mudman. She wondered if she could make it on her own with two kids. She had known a bunch of women that did. In a perfect case scenario, her children would grow up in a two parent household. She would be a soccer mom, and Mudman would work a regular nine to five to support the

family. But she already knew that they would never have a regular family. They were too deeply woven in the Underworld for that. Mudman was dead set on being king of the Game. She'd made her peace with that a long time ago.

"Mudman, if you don't tell me who dis bitch is, I'm 'bout to pull dis trigger. Den I'ma raise these children on my own. What is this bitch's name?" she screamed.

"I love you. Only you. Now let dat shit go."

That was it. Keisha couldn't take it no more. She took a step back, and began squeezing her trigger back to back with her eyes closed. She didn't want to see how the bullets were ripping Mudman's face apart. She couldn't believe that she was killing him, but she was. She pulled the trigger over and over.

Mudman stood there with a frown on his face as the gun clicked over and over. He had been the one to slip the .9 millimeter into Keisha's purse after unloading it once he decided that he was going to tell her about what happened between him and Ashley, though he had yet to expose Ashley. He knocked the gun out of her hand and slammed her into the wall. "Bitch, are you serious!" he snapped.

Keisha opened her eyes. Mudman didn't have a scar on his face. He was still intact. She wondered, how could that be? In her state of craziness, she'd not even paid attention to the fact that the gun hadn't emitted a sound, nor had it jumped in her hand. She grew remorseful. "Baby, I'm sorry. I was so mad. I kept imagining you and another bitch fucking and it became too much for me."

Mudman didn't know how to take what had just happened. Had she been anybody else, he would have filled her body with lead. He held her for a second, and then let her go. "Keisha, you lucky you is who you is. If you were anybody else, I would be torturing you right now, and I wouldn't be feeling

shit about it." He turned his back to her and slipped on his coat.

Keisha fixed her clothes. "Sure you thank you 'bout to go?" she asked, walking over to him.

"Don't worry about. I need to get as far away from yo' ass as I possibly can right now. I can't believe you just tried to smoke me. If I would have left them bullets in yo' gun, I would be a dead man right now."

Keisha stood there feeling like shit. "So you just finna leave me?"

He ignored her. He fixed his guns on his waist and situated his bulletproof vest. He took ahold of the door handle and unlocked it.

Keisha rushed over and slammed it close. "Mudman, you ain't finna leave me in dis hotel while you run da streets. You cheated on me, and I tried to slay yo' ass. We even. You need to stay here tonight so we can talk. I need to know what I've done wrong as a woman to make you go and seek the charms of somebody else. Please stay."

"It ain't got nothing to do wit' you doing somethin' wrong. I love you, shawty, but other pussy calls from time to time. I just ain't been picking up the phone. I fucked up one time, and you acting like it's the end of the world. Dat ain't cool." He pulled her off of the door and pushed her on to the bed. "I'll be back."

"Mudman, if you leave out of here tonight, I am too. I'm not finna sit around and be on lockdown while you fuck and run da streets like crazy. You supposed to be here wit' me. We in dis shit together."

Mudman looked her over. He felt saddened for a brief second. Then his heart turned blacker than a pile of wet mud. "Shid, what would you have done if there was bullets in that gun, and you would have killed me?" he snapped.

Keisha stood up. "Baby, but it wasn't. I just thank God in heaven that it wasn't. I would have taken my own life next."

Mudman waved her off. "What the fuck ever. I gotta attend to dis street bidness. I'll be back. I love you." Before she could answer him, he closed the door.

Keisha fell to her knees. She cried into her hands. She felt like she was losing Mudman. Even more than that, she felt like she was losing herself. She needed to get out of the room. She needed some fresh air. She needed to clear her head.

Hood Rich

Chapter 9

Prentice pulled the syringe out of the vein in the back of his hand. His eyes rolled backward. He closed his eyelids and smacked his lips. The drug coursed through his system and had him nodding in and out in a matter of minutes. He snored for two straight minutes, perked up, and looked across the street to the restaurant that he'd watched Keisha walk into beside Savanna. He didn't know who Savanna was, or where she had come from, and he didn't care. He would take care of her as well since she was with Keisha. The kill would mean nothing to him. He rubbed his nose, and scratched his injection sight. "I got you tonight, Keisha. I'ma kill you, and dat li'l yellow bitch you walking wit'," he grumbled before nodding back off. He had the outside of the restaurant surrounded with his Baton Rouge killas. He felt that there was no way Keisha was going to get away from him this time.

<center>***</center>

"So she was mad?" Ashley asked, giving Mudman a tall, cold glass of orange juice.

Mudman nodded. "I told you she tried to take me out da game. Had I not taken the bullets out of her gun, I wouldn't be sitting right hurr right now."

Ashley moaned. "Uh uh, and I would have been devastated. I need you, Mudman. You the realest man I have ever had in my life." She sat on his lap and wrapped her arm around his neck. "So are you ever going to tell her who I am?"

He downed a third of the contents and set the glass on the table. "Shawty, if she ever finds out dat you da one I'm fuckin', she gon' kill yo' ass. Keisha might be a female, but she'll take a nigga out da game as quick as a dude would. She been my right hand for a few years now so I know what it is."

Ashley felt jealous. She hated whenever Mudman gave Keisha a bunch of compliments. She felt that when he was in her presence that he should have been focused on the two of them, and no one else. "Well, daddy, I'm sorry that you had a horrible night so far, but you're here now. She straddled his lap. She held his shoulders and looked into his eyes. "I missed you."

Mudman nodded. "Here you go wit' dis shit." He looked off.

Ashley held his face. "Daddy, I missed you, and I love you." She leaned forward and kissed his lips for the first time.

Mudman had never allowed for her to kiss his lips. He felt that the act was too intimate. That the only person allowed to kiss his lips should been Keisha. But ever since Keisha had tried to kill him, his mind was all fucked up. He was still imagining himself laying on a slab in the morgue.

He returned her kisses and felt his nature rise. He held her small waist and tongued her down. He picked her up and crashed into the wall with her. "I'm finna hit dis pussy again. Fuck it. You finna give me some of dis fresh shit." He let her down.

Ashley walked sexily to the couch. Once there, she looked back over her shoulders at him and hiked up her red lace night gown, exposing her nakedness. "Come get you some of dis pussy, daddy." She bent over the arm and ran her hand between her thighs. Her pussy felt like it was on fire.

Mudman stripped to his boxers. He walked over to her, stroking his piece. As soon as he was close enough he slid it into her, and didn't wait to step on the gas. He got to fucking her at full speed like a crazed savage, hitting that pussy hard, long stroking.

Ashley grabbed the throw pillow and bit into it. She screamed as Mudman fucked her with reckless abandon. His

dick felt like it was deep inside of her stomach. "Daddy! Daddy! Slow down! Unn! Unn! Unn! Daddy!"

He yanked her back to him. The more he watched his piece slide in and out of her, the angrier he became. He got to killing Ashley, growling like a lion. Her pussy felt tighter than before. Tighter, and she was twice as wet.

Ashley arched her back and came. She beat her fist into the couch and slammed back into him again and again. Her pussy belonged to him. Couldn't nobody hit it like Mudman, she felt. She looked over her left shoulder to see Mudman staring between their thrusting sexes. That turned her on, for some reason. She slapped her on ass. "Uh! Spank yo' baby, daddy. Spank me! Please!"

Mudman slapped her ass and dug her out. Her ass jiggled and wobbled as he broke her off. He slapped it over and over. Each cheek took a bruising simultaneously. When he felt her shaking under him, he came hard, skeeting into her walls.

Ashley felt it. She slammed back as hard as she could on him, milking his pole. His jets brought on another orgasm from herself. She stuffed her face into the throw pillow and screamed hard, biting on it. She dropped it and breathed heavily.

Mudman pulled out and picked her up. She wrapped her thick thighs around him. He slid back in and bounced her up and down. "Tell. Me. Who. Hitting. Dis. Pussy?" He bounced her higher and higher.

"My daddy! My daddy! Uhhhh! Shit! My dadd-deeee!" She came again, harder than before.

Mudman fell to the carpet with her stroking away. He was dead set on fucking her until his dick gave out. He was on two Percocet sixties and three capsules of pink Mollie. He planned on being deep in Ashley's womb for a long time.

Mars held his ear to the door of Ashley's apartment and cursed under his breath. He knew they had been fucking all along. He shook his head. Suddenly he hated Mudman. He wanted to not only take his life, but he wanted him to suffer in the worst way imaginable. Ashley would pay too, he vowed. She would pay for casting him to the side. She would regret all of her decisions real soon. He stepped away from the door and adjusted his boner. His mind was overridden with sucka shit.

Keisha looked across the table at Savanna. She still couldn't believe how beautiful her goddaughter was. She watched the girl pick at her steak. She seemed as if something was wrong with her. "What's the matter, Savanna, you not hungry?"

Savanna dropped her fork. "It's not that I'm not hungry, it's that I can tell something is wrong with you. Do you wanna talk about it?"

Keisha shifted uncomfortably. She gazed out into the Steak House. It was packed. The majority of the tables had two or three people stuffing their faces. They appeared to be having polite conversations. The ones that weren't having conversations were either chewing the food with their eyes closed or they were waiting to get their food. She ran her fingers through her hair, which was something she did whenever she was stressed out. It was a habit of hers. She exhaled loudly and looked across the table. "I don't know, baby, you might be a li'l too young for me to discuss my problems with you."

"You already know that I'm wise beyond my years. You tell me that all the time." She reached across the table and took ahold of her hand. "Talk to me, mama, I'm here for you."

Keisha slumped her shoulders. "It's Mudman. He cheated on me for the first time during our relationship." Keisha didn't know why she told Savanna that, but she had. She honestly needed a safe place to open up with her thoughts. Though Savanna was only seventeen, she was curious to hear what the girl was going to say.

Savanna squeezed her hand harder. "Well, I don't know why he would do something like that when he has a bad as woman like you. You're past a dime. I guess he didn't get the memo."

Keisha laughed. "Thank you, baby."

"No, I'm serious, mama. If I were a dude, I would be happily faithful to you. I think it's just in men's DNA to sleep around. I certainly wouldn't blame myself for this, and you shouldn't either. If you want, we can go back to the hotel right now and get a little even. I'll do whatever you want, and let you party with me as well."

Now Keisha was blushing. She laughed Savanna off. "Girl, you definitely are wise beyond your years."

Savanna frowned. "I just care about you." She slid around the booth and wrapped her arm around Keisha's neck. She kissed her cheek. "So what do you say, beautiful? You wanna go back and take your mind off of Mudman?" She rubbed Keisha's thighs slipped her hand between them and brushed over her pussy lips through the material of her panties.

Keisha opened her thighs wider, and moaned. She imagined Savanna's perfect young body underneath her clothes, and felt some type of way. "Yeah, Princess, let's get up out of here."

Savanna pressed the material into Keisha's slit. She rubbed it around in a circular motion. "Dat sounds like a plan to me. I want you all to myself anyway. Come on, mama. Let's bounce."

Ashley scooted back into Mudman's lap as they spooned on the bed. Her middle was aching. He'd screwed her for three hours straight. She was spent, yet happy that he was lying next to her. He wrapped his bicep around her protectively.

"Daddy, if it was up to me, I would stay like this forever." She smiled and imagined the possibility of that.

Mudman was exhausted. He didn't wanna talk. All he wanted to do was to hold her while he got his mind right. "Shawty, take yo' ass to sleep before I beat that pussy in some more," he threatened.

She giggled. "Okay, good night."

Mudman closed his eyes. His conscience was getting the better of him. He couldn't help but feel like he was somehow betraying Keisha. He started to feel as if he were rotting in the inside. He sat up in bed. "Shawty, hand me my phone."

"Wait. What?"

"Li'l mama, you heard what I said. Hand me my phone. It's on the dresser over there." He pointed.

Ashley got out of the bed and grabbed his phone. She handed it to him. "Huh. I thought we was finna go to sleep."

"We is, after I call Keisha." He hit her number.

Ashley crossed her arms and rolled her eyes. "Dang, daddy, you fuckin' up a good night. I felt like I was in Paradise for a minute."

"Bitch, shut up, it's ringing," Mudman ordered.

Ashley felt her feelings being stepped on. She walked out of the room and down the hallway. When she got to the living room, she sat on the couch and lowered her head. It wasn't lowered for more than three seconds before she was snatched from the couch with a hand placed over her mouth.

Keisha slammed the door to her Bentley truck. She clicked the lock for Savanna to get inside. Savanna got inside and closed her door. As soon as it was closed, she leaned across the console and pulled Keisha to her. They locked lips and kissed loudly. Tongues wrestled and played over one another's. When Savanna pulled back, Keisha's nipples were aching.

Savanna hiked up her skirt. "Looks you got me all wet." She pulled her panties down and separated her sex lips with her fingers.

Keisha saw her sheen. She could smell her pussy just a hint as well. It made her purr. "Okay, baby, we gotta get back to the hotel. I got something special for you." She didn't know what she could come up with to make things special. All she knew was that she couldn't wait to get a piece of Savanna.

Savanna slid two fingers into herself and worked them in and out. "Mama, can you pull yours up a li'l bit so I can see how thick yo' thighs is again. You always drive me crazy." She sucked on her bottom lip.

Keisha wiggled from side to side in her seat. She pulled her skirt up as far as she could before starting the engine and pulling out of the lot. She looked over to Savanna. The girl was going to town on herself at full speed.

Savanna eyed Keisha's chocolate thighs. The size of them drove her out of her mind. Keisha's body was perfect to her.

She dropped down to the floor and sucked all over Keisha's thighs while she drove. She pulled the right one away from the left one, and stuffed her face into her box. Before Keisha even knew it was happening, her panties were pulled down to her ankles and Savanna was eating her like a seasoned veteran. She bucked into her face and kept rolling.

Savanna's fingers shot in and out of herself. She imagined that they were Keisha's. She pulled on her clit with her lips and came listening to Keisha struggled to suppress her own orgasm.

Keisha swerved in traffic. She entered onto the highway and stepped on the gas. "Baby, just wait til we get there please. You gon' fuck around and make me crash."

Savanna laughed and ran her tongue over her lips. She took her seat and continued to rub herself. "I want you so bad, Keisha. You so damn fine. I hope I can grow into a body like yours." Two fingers sank deeply into her channel.

Keisha shivered. "Li'l girl, you driving me crazy. We finna have one hell of a night."

"I hope so. All I been thinking about since you picked me up was just us being alone so I could - "

BOOWAH!

Savanna's head exploded. Her brains splashed all across the windshield. It looked like bloody chitterlings. She fell to the floor of the truck and began to shake.

Keisha swerved the truck and almost crashed into a guard railing. She couldn't see; the entire windshield was covered in blood. She started to scream. She looked down at Savanna and then over her shoulder. She already knew what had happened before she saw him.

Prentice laughed at the top of his lungs. He pressed the Mossberg to the back of Keisha's head. "Shawty, I told you that you would never get away from me. We finna have a

whole lot of fun. Get off on dat exit up there, and don't utter a word."

Keisha could feel her heart pounding in her chest. She was shaking. She felt like she couldn't breathe. Then her cell phone began to vibrate on her lap. She knew it could be no-body other than Mudman calling her. The thought made her even sicker to her stomach. She needed him.

Hood Rich

Chapter 10

Mudman came out of the bedroom to see why Ashley wasn't answering him. He'd called out to her three times. As he stepped into the living room, he saw that it was packed with gunmen. A masked Miguelito stood behind Ashley with his hand over her mouth. Mudman got ready to run back to the room to grab his gun when Miguelito called out to him. "Mudman, it's of no use. We didn't come to hurt you, or her."

Mudman didn't give a fuck what Miguelito was talking about. He grabbed his Glocks and slowly made his way back into the room. Once there, he aimed his guns as the intruders. "What the fuck y'all want?"

Miguelito threw Ashley to the floor in front of Mudman. He pulled off his mask. "Listen to me, friend. I have been sent to you by The Bull."

When Miguelito revealed who he was, Mudman became even angrier. "How da fuck did you get past my security?"

Miguelito laughed. "Dem Project kids that you got out there holding machine guns? Man, it wasn't that hard." He took a seat on the couch.

Ashley crawled to her feet and stood behind Mudman. "How the fuck did y'all get in my house?"

Miguelito held up a master key. "Oh, the Super of dis building works for us."

"Nall, muthafucka he works for me," Mudman said, pointing to himself.

Miguelito giggled. "Man, Mudman, you are tripping. Bro, you ain't shit when it comes to the Sinaloas. They run the muthafuckin' world. We all are just working for them when it's all said and done."

Mudman mugged him. "What the fuck The Bull want wit' me?"

Miguelito looked up at him. "It appears that you took a major hit dis week. The Bull is concerned that your loss could affect his finances, and if that is the case, unfortunately I'ma have to take you so we can face him head on."

"Take me? Where the fuck you think you finna take me?" Mudman stepped forward, ready to blow Miguelito back. He already felt offended because the man had entered his side bitch's house without his permission. Secondly, he'd said that the Super belonged to him. Thirdly, Mudman felt like he was trying to treat him like a bitch. He wasn't going for it. He'd rather meet death then to let any man treat him less than a King.

Miguelito crossed his legs. "Mudman, you do understand that I brought you into this high level of dope slanging, right? Do you understand that if you do not have The Bull's money at your deadline that not only is he going to torture and kill you, but he'll handle me right after you?"

"Bruh, why da fuck you talking like I done fell off or something? I still got my shit under control. I ain't gotta hit The Bull until next Friday," Mudman spat, ready to snatch Miguelito off of the couch and make him choke on the barrel of his gun.

"So you sure you're going to have eight hundred thousand dollars? That's no problem for you?" Miguelito asked, flicking a piece of lint off of his pants.

"Dat's what I'm telling yo' ass. Now get the fuck out of my bitch's shit, and don't brang yo' monkey ass back into these buildings without coming to me first. You got dat?"

Miguelito rose from the couch. "I left a present for you in the bathroom." He snapped his fingers. He and his men left Ashley's apartment.

She rushed and wrapped her arms around him. "I thought they was finna kill us. I swear to God, I thought they were."

Mudman nudged her off of him. He took off to her bathroom. He opened the door and stood back. Inside of the tub were three of the four men that Mudman had put in charge of watching the hallway. They were bound and gagged. The only one missing appeared to be Mars. Mudman felt angry. He grabbed the shower curtain and took a pistol off of his hip, handing it to Ashley. "Bitch, come here. Look at dese niggas."

Ashley stepped into the bathroom and looked into the tub. She felt disgusted at the sight of the men. "Dat's pathetic."

Mudman clenched his jaw. He pulled the shower curtain around them but kept both he and Ashley inside of it. "Finger fuck dat ma'fucka till it's empty. Bitch, I ain't playing either. Dese niggas don't deserve to live. You ready, baby?"

Ashley buttered up. "Yep."

"Let's go!"

Boom! Boom! Boom! Boom! Boom! The guns jumped in their hands. Blood popped up and wet the shower curtains. They kept on shooting until their clips were empty. The bathroom smelled like gunpowder and blood.

Mudman washed his hands in the sink and called Mars. He wanted to know why he'd left his post without permission.

Prentice slammed Keisha against the brick wall of the basement and held her in place. His henchmen took her wrists and bound them in chains over her head. They slapped shackles on her ankles as well. When they were finished, Prentice ordered them out of the basement. "Don't nobody come down hurr unless I give you permission. Me and dis bitch got some serious bidness that need tending to."

Keisha tried to free herself from the chains. She hollered into the duct tape. Sweat slid down her forehead. She felt sick and ready to panic.

Prentice walked up to her and grabbed her by the mouth. He squeezed it as hard as he could and leaned into her ear. "I'm 'bout to take dis hurr tape off of yo' mouth so I can ask you a few questions. If you scream or try anythang dumb, bitch, I'm offing you. It's as simple as dat. Nod yo' ma'fuckin' head if you understanding me right now?"

Keisha slowly nodded her head. She swallowed her spit. She was trying her best to look for an escape route. The basement was standard. It was covered by brick walls. It had a low ceiling. The light bulb was red. It felt stuffy. The heat was on ninety. It was sweltering. Prentice had turned the heat up that high on purpose. He knew that Keisha hated when it was too hot.

Prentice yanked the tape from her mouth. "Breathe, hoe."

Keisha took in a deep breath. It felt like a mini slice of heaven. She swallowed her spit again. "Prentice, why won't you leave me the fuck alone?"

Prentice laughed. "Bitch, you got some explaining to do. He stepped into her face and sniffed it. "Mmm, you smell real fine, Keisha. Just like always." He licked the side of her face and stood back to look her over.

Keisha cringed. She closed her eyes until he was finished, then she opened them. "What the fuck do you want from me?"

He grabbed her throat. "Bitch, I done already told you about dat. Now dis is yo' last warning. Don't let it happen again." He squeezed her throat and pushed her backward into the brick wall with his hand, releasing her.

Keisha coughed and struggled to breathe for a few seconds. "Dis shit ain't right, Prentice. We supposed to be even. You killed my mother. You killed Kayla. You killed Sandra. You killed Savanna. You killed everybody that I cared about in dis life. What do you want from me?"

"Not everybody. I still gotta perform an autopsy on Mudman. Speaking of which, whatever made you cheat on me with dat nigga?" He stroked her curly hair.

Keisha curled her nose. "You was on dem drugs real tough, Prentice. You didn't give a fuck about me no more. All you cared about was dat heroin. You treated me like shit, and you know it."

"Bitch, so dat gives you a reason to go and fuck my cousin? Dat gives you a reason to get pregnant wit' his baby? Dat gives you the reason to try to kill me beside this nigga?" He grabbed a handful of her hair and yanked it as hard as he could.

Keisha screamed, but caught herself before she screamed too loud. She felt her lacefront being ripped from her head. The braiding prevented it from coming all the way off.

Prentice slung the hair to the floor. "You gon' have to give me a better answer then dat."

Keisha's head was pounding. She didn't know what to say or do. She needed Mudman. She hated him for walking out on her. Had he stayed in their hotel room, Savanna would still be alive. She would never be stuck inside of the impossible predicament. She honestly felt that way.

"You always had a thing for him, didn't you?" Prentice closed the distance between them and slid his hand between her thighs. The way she was bound, they were spaced apart just right for him to do so. He slipped his hand into her panties and cuffed her monkey. "Answer my question."

Keisha felt like she wanted to throw up. Since she had been with Mudman, no other man had been able to touch her. She felt as if she was violating him on a major scale.

Prentice slipped two rough fingers into her. "Answer me!"

"No, I didn't! Heh! Heh! Heh! Stop! Puh! Puh! Leese!" she cried.

Prentice ignored her and kept jugging. "Why you fuck him den? Why you choose him over me?" He pulled his fingers out and sucked them into his mouth, savoring the flavor of Keisha.

"He came on to me. Right while you were dozing off of that Tar shit. He came at me, and things went from there."

"But you couldn't have said no, huh? You couldn't tell dat nigga to get the fuck away from you because you was in love with me, huh?" He pulled out his piece. It was erect. He stepped to her and ground it up against her panty front.

Keisha felt like throwing up on him. "It ain't happen like you thank, Prentice? Why you just can't let dat shit go? What's done is done."

Prentice yanked her panties to the side and then ripped them violently off of her body. He rubbed her naked sex and looked at it as if he were seeing it for the first time. "Yeah, well, we gon' see what you saying when I get done wit' dis pussy." He lined himself up and slid deep into her box.

She groaned. "No!"

Prentice went to town. He sucked her neck and held her ass. In and out. In and out. "Dis. Was. My. Pussy. Keisha. Uh. Uh. Uh. Mine!" he roared, and went berserk, fucking as fast as he could.

Keisha closed her eyes and died inside. She imagined that he was Mudman. She escaped to an island where it was just Mudman and herself. They were celebrating the arrival of their twins and their marriage. Though he was told by the doctor to stay away from her lowers for six weeks, he couldn't stay away, so he took to pounding her out on the beach. On top of white sand while the children stayed with their nanny.

Prentice ripped her dress and released her right breast, suckling the hard nipple. He bit into it and tried his best to pull it from the mound. Keisha's pussy felt tight as a fist and wet

as a pool. He missed it. He had plans on using it as much as he wanted to while he held her. He lifted the dress all the way up and came when he saw her baby bump.

Keisha felt him splashing into her and she fainted on her feet. She felt so disgusted that she wanted to die. The last thing she wanted to have inside of her body was his seed. "Please get off of me, Prentice."

Prentice staggered backwards. "Bitch, you pregnant again? Huh?" He wiped his mouth with the back of his hands. His pants were around his ankles. His piece still rock hard with semen leaking from it along with her secretions. He pointed at her belly. "You are, aren't you?"

Keisha cringed. She started to panic. "Yes, Prentice. You took out last child, and God is blessing us with these."

His eyes got big. "Dese? Bitch, it's two in dere?" he hollered.

Keisha started praying in her head. She didn't know what else to do. She prayed for the safety of her unborn children. She prayed for God to deliver her away from Prentice. She prayed for Mudman to rescue her. She prayed for it all to be a dream. She just wanted it to be over. She begged the Lord to save her.

Prentice pulled up his pants and fixed them. He grabbed the gun from the washing machine and placed it to her belly. "Not on my watch, Keisha. You supposed to have my shawty. You was my baby mama. I called you dat. I'll never let you have a family wit' dis nigga. Over my dead body." He cocked the hammer, and took a step back.

Boom! Boom! Boom! Boom!

Hood Rich

Chapter 11

Prentice ducked down and went for cover behind the washing machine. "What the fuck was that?" he snapped.

Keisha had her eyes closed. She prayed it was God answering her prayers. She slowly opened them. She took a deep breath and refused to cry. She would never allow for Prentice to see tears coming out of her eyes on his account. She'd rather die first.

Boom! Boom! Boom! Boom!

Prentice stood up and ran up the steps. He stopped and came back down them. "Bitch, keep yo' mouth closed. Don't test me!" he warned. He rushed back up the stairs as more gunfire ensued. He looked to see his men taking cover. There were two vans parked in back of their apartment building. Shooters stood in front of them, spitting machine guns. His troops fired back. Prentice closed the back door and nearly fell down the stairs. He didn't know what was going on. "Stay yo' ass right there. I'll be back for you in a minute," he ordered Keisha.

Keisha wanted to yell for him to go fuck himself. But instead, she ignored him. She closed her eyes and started to pray again.

Prentice eased up the back steps and into his trap. He ran into the middle room, where he kept his assault rifles. He grabbed a Draco and slammed a hundred round magazine inside of it. He cocked it and ran out the front door into the night. Gunfire continued to ensue. He hopped over the neighbor's fence and ran along their gangway. When he got into their backyard, he kept on running. He stopped just before he hit the alley and peeked around the side of the garage. He saw four men standing in front of the two opened vans. They were bucking Mach .10s at his crew with no regard. They wore

black masks over their faces. Their arms were brown. He figured them to be some form of Spanish. Immediately, he began to think Cartel.

He ducked down and eased slightly out into the alley. He aimed the Draco and began firing rapidly. The Draco jumped in his hands. He watched two of the men vibrate on their feet as the bullets ate at their flesh. They dropped to the ground with blood gushing out of them. Prentice kept on shooting.

Keisha pulled down as hard as she could on the cuffs. She had already gotten her left hand free. She jimmied the lock to her shackles by use of a bobby pin from her lacefront, popping them easily. Now she had to free her right hand. She pulled down, and dropped her bodyweight. Her hand began to bleed. The skin peeled backward. She pulled, and yanked it free, falling to her knees. "Thank you God!" she cried out. Now tears were running down her cheeks. She wiped them and ran for the stairs on bare feet. She could feel Prentice's cum leaking out of her middle. It made her sick to the stomach. She climbed the steps as more gunfire ensued. When she got to the very top, she ran through the house. She stopped as she got into the front room and saw the door open. There was a plate of food on table. A big porter house steak sat on the plate with a baked potato and carrots. She grabbed the knife from the plate and continued on her path. She eased open the door just as a car slammed on its brakes directly in front of the house. She pushed the door closed a bit, and hid behind it.

The driver jumped out and made his way up the steps. He pushed open the door and came inside. "Prentice! Where da fuck you at, mane?" He stepped further inside. He was about to walk into the living room when he saw Keisha move from

the corner of his eye. He reached for his .40, but before he could raise it, Keisha rushed him and slammed the knife into his throat. She dropped down and head-butted him in the nuts. He flew backward, landing hard on the couch before rolling to the floor.

Keisha grabbed the knife out of his throat. A rush of blood poured out of him. He sounded like he was choking on it. Keisha picked up his gun and ran outside. She jumped into his car and stormed away from the curb, crying. Once again, God had been merciful.

<p style="text-align: center;">***</p>

Prentice stood over the wounded shooter. He held his hands up. His body was riddled with bullets, yet he still held on. Prentice yanked off his mask to reveal a Mexican's face. He bonked him upside the head with the handle of his rifle. "Who do you work for?"

The Mexican spit up blood. He winced in agony and laid out flat on the ground. His body shook three times before he laid still. Prentice knelt down and looked him over by use of the moonlight. He confirmed his death. He stood up. "Get rid of dat muthafucka, and clean up dis mess. We out of here in ten minutes," he said to his men. They went right into action following his commands.

Prentice hustled inside of the trap. He hurried to the basement. When he stepped off of the last stair, he saw Keisha's chains still in place, but she was nowhere to be found. He hollered as loud as he could. "Fuckin' bitch! How da fuck she do dis!" He rushed to the chains and looked them over. He saw pieces of her skin around the handcuffs. He picked out the skin and ate it. His obsession of her had become sickening. He looked over the entire area and still couldn't, for the life of

him understand how she had managed to make her escape. He walked back over to the chains and sniffed them up. Then he was laughing at the top of his lungs.

"I don't know what the fuck going on wit' Lainey, man. She ain't never did no shit like dis before. She been gone four days. Linda going crazy, cuz," Pooty said, handing Figgady the liter bottle of water that he'd dropped four Percocets into.

Figgady took the bottle and turned it up. He was already gone off of two grams of Sinaloa Tar. He felt numb. His eyelids were heavy as anvils. "Shawty probably out wit' one of her boyfriends or something, mane. You know how teenagers get when they get to going through that awkward phase."

"I'll beat her li'l ass. She just turned fifteen. She bet' not be out there messing wit' none of them li'l ratchet-ass niggas," Pooty snapped. He imagined Lainey in one of the many trap houses around Compton, and it pissed him off. He knew better than that. He didn't think that she would ever do something as negligent as that. She was a good girl. "She too innocent for all that kind of shit, Figgady. She just a kid."

Figgady laughed. "She might have been one age, but shawty li'l ass definitely wasn't shaped like one. She looked like a grown-ass woman." He turned the bottle up again and handed it out to Pooty.

Pooty stared at him for a second, then slowly took the bottle from him. "Mane, I been knowing that li'l girl since she was two years old. She always looked like a child to me. I can't believe you would even say she didn't." He wiped his mouth and set the liter of water on the table in the den. Suddenly he didn't feel like drinking it anymore. All of his attention was on his cousin. He decided to pick Figgady's brain a

bit to see what kind of a man he was actually dealing with. They had been away from each other for so long that it was possible that Figgady had turned into a creep. Pooty rubbed his chin. "But den again, now dat I think about it, Lainey is kinda thick though, huh?"

Figgady nodded out for a second. When he heard Pooty say these words, he came to. "What you say?"

Pooty scooted to the edge of the couch. "I said Lainey is thick though. She be walking around in them li'l-ass shorts all the time. Sometimes it be taking her more than a few minutes to squeeze into her jeans because every time we buy her some new ones, she wind up bussing out of them real quick. But am I tripping? She is thick, right?"

Figgady felt his piece jump. He grabbed it, and then took his hand away as if it had been placed on a hot stove. "Hell yeah, she was strapped. That's the first thing I noticed when you introduced me to her. I didn't really wanna pay attention though because I didn't know how old she was. But she was most definitely strapped though."

Pooty felt his heart drop. "So you did notice, huh?" He laughed it off. He needed to do some more digging. He had a feeling that Figgady knew what was going on with Lainey. He didn't know exactly what was up with her, but something just kept nagging at him and telling him that Figgady knew where she was. Maybe he was trying to cover for her, he thought.

"Yeah, I noticed, but like I said, I didn't know how old she was so I stopped paying attention," he lied. He closed his eyes and began to nod some more.

Pooty eyed him closely. He wanted to dig further. He wanted to flat out ask Figgady if he knew where Lainey was, and if they had messed around since he'd been staying with him. But he was sure that would cause an argument, and possibly even a fight between the two of them. So he had to be

smarter than that. He cleared his throat to wake Figgady up out of his heroin-induced slumber.

Linda stepped to the door and was about to knock on it when she heard Pooty clear his throat. She set the basket of laundry down on the floor and placed her ear to the door. She frowned as she heard Pooty began to talk again.

"I'm saying, Figgady, you telling me that when you saw Lainey walking around in dem li'l shorts that you was worried about her age more than that fat ass she was carrying? Come on now, it used to drive me crazy. I know you had to be going through it. I peeped how you used to look at her."

Figgady was no idiot. He knew that Pooty was fishing now. He figured that he had to have suspected some sort of foul play. He knew he had to finesse him. Figgady slid to the edge of the sofa. "Nigga, I don't give a fuck if she was of age. I got too much love and respect for you to ever cross those lines with that baby. Ever since I been out here, you and Linda been holding me down. I owe both of y'all the utmost loyalty. I hope Lainey comes home soon." He sat back and picked up the remote control, turning the television to Sports Center.

Pooty looked him over and wondered if he was telling the truth. He had given him no reason to believe that he wasn't. He decided to drop the matter. "Yeah, a'ight, Figgady, I appreciate that."

Linda busted through the door and fell to her knees in tears. "They found her! Oh my God! They found my li'l sister!" she screamed.

Pooty jumped up. "What the fuck you mean they found her?"

Linda cried into her hands. They found her four blocks over in a dumpster, Pooty. They say she dead. Somebody killed her." She rocked back and forth, crying harder and harder.

Figgady jumped up and staggered on his feet. He didn't know what to do or say. He thought that the garbage men would have been done their jobs. How was it so many days later and they were just finding her body, Figgady wondered. "Why the fuck would anybody do dat?" he asked.

Pooty ignored him. He fell to the ground and wrapped his arms around Linda. "Baby, it's okay. It's okay. I'm pretty sure this is all a mistake."

Linda shook her head. "No, it's not. It's not! They fuckin' found her body. They did. Why did they?" she cried.

Pooty held her, confused. Though he could hear the words coming out of her mouth, he still couldn't understand how they could be factual. Who would want to hurt Lainey? She was the sweetest little girl in the world.

Linda allowed him to hold her for a few moments, then she pushed him off of her. She jumped up and ran out of the room. "I gotta go make sure it's her. Lord, please don't let it be my little sister," she wailed.

Pooty stood up and was dumbfounded. It was taking a long time for the reality of the situation to register to him. "You think it's her?" he asked Figgady.

Figgady was still high as a kite. He forced his eyelids open. "She sounded pretty sho'. I hope not doe. Ma'fuckas ain't have no right to kill her and throw her in a dumpster like that. What the fuck is the world coming too?" He picked up the bottle of water and drank from it.

Pooty looked at him from the corners of his eyes. "Come on, man, we gotta go down there to see what's good."

Figgady shook his head in defiance. "Nigga, hell nall. You know how many police finna be down there? I got all types of warrants and shit. I'll wait for y'all right here. I mean, I pray it ain't true about what she saying, but still and all, I gotta be smart."

Pooty nodded. "Right." He stood there in silence for what seemed like a long time. Finally, he left the room. He found Linda in the hallway laid out flat on her back. She was knocked out cold. His eyes got as big as planets. He rushed to her side. "Baby, baby, what's the matter?"

Linda was unresponsive. Her blood pressure had been raised so high that she wound up passing out. Her brain had momentarily shut down. She shook on the floor. Saliva seeped out of the corner of her mouth.

Pooty placed his ear to her chest to see if he could hear her heart heating. Once he confirmed the rapid beat, he sighed in relief. He picked her up and set her on the couch. "Baby, wake up. Are you okay?"

Linda opened her eyes. As soon as she saw his face, she began to cry. "Please tell me it was a dream. Please, Pooty."

There was a loud knocking on the door. Pooty perked up. He could hear the walkie talkies of the officers who stood outside on the porch. He knew what that meant. "Look, baby, the police out there. You gotta go answer the door. I gotta go. You already know I can't be here right now.

"Don't leave me, Pooty. I can't do this on my own. Please, I'm begging you," Linda whimpered.

The banging of the police intensified. "Los Angeles Police Department, anybody home?"

Pooty kissed her forehead. "I love you, baby. Be strong." He took off running out the back door. Figgady had already left out of the same exit.

Linda fell to her knees and cried as hard as she could while the officers beat on the door. She couldn't believe that any of this was happening, and worst of all that Pooty had left her to fend for herself. She felt that something wasn't right about that.

Chapter 12

Mudman stepped into the hotel suite and saw the room was in total darkness. He glanced at the clock on his cell phone, and saw that it read three-forty in the morning. Lightning flashed across the sky, illuminating the room for a split second. He saw Keisha's image sitting up on the bed. He felt a twinge of guilt after leaving Ashley's apartment, knowing all that they had done. He took a deep breath. He didn't feel like dealing with her emotions. Tomorrow was a new day. "Look, shawty, I know you got some shit on yo' mind, but dat shit can wait until the morning. I'm tired, and I been through hell tonight." He pulled off his shirt and tossed it over the chair that was on the side of their king-sized bed.

"Where were you?" Keisha asked softly. She wiped the tears from her cheeks.

"Keisha, I ain't got time for dat shit right now. We'll talk about all of dat in da morning. Didn't you just hear what I said?"

Keisha rocked back and forth and cried into her fist. She sniffled. "Where were you, Mudman! Where the fuck was you! You were supposed to protect me!" she screamed, falling to her knees.

Mudman turned on the light to see what was going on. He saw her hunched into a ball on the floor, rocking back and forth, and he began to panic. Her hair was ripped out of her head. Her dress was also ripped. She has half-naked. There was blood on her wrists. He figured she'd tried to kill herself. "Keisha, what the fuck happened?"

"He raped me. He raped me, and you wasn't there to protect me. You left me to fend for myself. I will never forgive you for this, Mudman. I will never forgive you for leaving me out in the cold like this." She cried harder.

Mudman was irate. "Raped you? Who da fuck raped you?"

Keisha pushed him away from her and stood up. "It don't matter. I need some money so I can get the fuck up out of here. I can't be around you anymore. You disgust me." She grabbed her suitcase out of the closet and proceeded to pack it.

Now Mudman could see that her dress was completely destroyed. She had blood all over her legs, and hands. Her face was swollen as if she'd been beaten. His mind couldn't fathom who would do such a thing, especially after knowing who she belonged to. "Baby, what the fuck happened?"

She continued to pack her things. "Don't worry about it. It doesn't concern you anymore. Go back to whatever bitch you been spending all dis time wit'. Wit' yo' trifling ass. I hate you. I should have never crossed over to you. You've hurt me so bad, Mudman," she whimpered. Her bottom lip began to twitch.

Mudman snatched her up. "Stop talking dis dumb shit. Who da fuck did dis shit to you? Huh?" He shook her. "Tell me!"

Keisha remained stoic. She stared at him without blinking. "If you don't get yo' fuckin' nasty-ass hands off of me, I am going to make you kill me. Get yo' hands off of me, and give me some money so I can leave this city tonight! Now, Mudman! Now!" she screamed.

This caught Mudman off guard. He snapped. He grabbed her by her arms and picked her up into the air. He held her there. "Keisha, tell me who da fuck did dis shit to you. Who raped you? Who ripped yo' clothes and shit up like dis?"

Keisha looked down on him. "The same ma'fucka that kilt Sandra, and now Savanna. The same person that murdered both of our parents. The same ma'fucka that's playing wit' us because you're too fuckin' weak to find him and kill him. Dis

is all yo' fault. You should have just left me alone. You should have never pursued me. Now we're being hunted."

Mudman let her down and turned his back to her. "Prentice? Dis ma'fucka did dis shit to you?" He looked at her over his shoulder. "How you know he killed Savanna?"

"Because he blew her fucking head off right in my face while I was driving my truck. I don't know where she and the truck is now because he ripped me from it at gunpoint. Before he put me in his basement and did what he wanted with me. Had I not escaped, he was going to kill me. And where the fuck were you? Wit' some bitch, right?" Keisha slumped to a seated position. "I can't believe you."

Mudman sat on the bed. First his traps had been hit. He was down seven hundred and twenty thousand dollars. Every penny of that was owed to the Sinaloas. To The Bull himself. He had less than two weeks and then the original Blood Thirsty Cartel would be coming for his and Keisha's lives. If that wasn't bad enough, he heard that Nike was set to be released from prison in two days. Word was that Nike was coming for the throne of Oakland. It had been his prior to his incarceration, and he wanted it back. That was going to prove to be a problem for Mudman. He knew that it was impossible to war and to make up the money that he needed to keep The Bull off of his ass at the same time. He had to figure things out, and quick. Then to find out that Prentice was lurking, hunting him and Keisha, was enough to drive him insane. He felt like he was losing his mind. For the first time in a long time, he felt like he was losing it. He didn't know now much more he could take.

Keisha stood up. "Why are you treating me like dis, Mudman? Haven't I been loyal to you? Haven't I devoted my entire life to you ever since we chose to cross those lines?"

He nodded. "Yeah, baby. You have."

"Then why are you doing me like this? Out of all people, why me?" She wiped tears from her cheeks again.

Mudman lowered his head. "I'm fucking up, Keisha. I feel like I'm losing my head. I thank I'm in too deep." He sighed and felt sick to his stomach.

Keisha felt her knees go weak. She never thought she would see the day when Mudman admitted that he was growing weaker. She always looked to him for strength. She always felt in the bottom of her heart that if any mam could conquer the impossible, then he was the man for the job. Mudman was her strength in times of weaknesses. But to hear him speak in a dejected fashion made Keisha drop to her knees again. "What do we do? What do we do, Mudman? Please tell me that you got a plan?"

Mudman took a deep breath. He slowly exhaled. "I don't know what I'ma do yet, but I gotta figure shit out soon. I'm just a li'l lost right now." He ran his hand over his face. "Come here."

Keisha continued to sit on the floor. She sniffled. "Why?"

Mudman kept his head lowered. His eyes began to get watery. He held his head back and took a deep breath. "Keisha, brang yo' ass hurr, mane, damn."

Keisha heard the way his voice was breaking up. She came to her feet and stood in front of him. "What you want, Mudman?"

Mudman looked into her face. Tears seeped out of his eyes, dripped down his cheeks. He reached out and grabbed her to him. He could smell the heavy odor of sex resonating from her body. It made him feel weaker. "I failed you, Keisha. I said I wouldn't never be one of dese bitch-ass niggas, and I wound up turning into one any way. I'm sorry, boo. Please know that with everythang that I am as a man that I am sorry."

He pulled her to him and wrapped her in his big arms. From this close, the scents of her assault were overpowering.

Keisha broke into tears even harder. As much has she hated Mudman in the moment, she loved him even more than what she could have ever imagined. He was the love of her life. She knew he wasn't perfect. She knew that he had a long way to go before he could be considered a saint. But he was her man, and she felt that he was really crazy about her with all things considered. "He hurt me, Mudman. He hurt me so bad, baby." She hugged him as tight as she could.

Mudman felt her shaking. He allowed for the tears to come out of him. They were long overdue. He had not shed tears since he was a little kid. He'd been through so many tragedies, heartaches, and pains, yet a tear never came from his eyes until this night. He could not stop the flow of them. He felt like he was breaking. "Keisha, I love you, boo, with all of my heart. I swear to God, on my mother's grave, that I will never do anything to hurt you again. I don't know how I got side tracked, but I did, baby. I felt like I was missing something. I should have never stepped outside of us. I'll never do dat shit again."

Keisha held him. "I believe you, baby. I believe you and I forgive you. Just hold me, Mudman. Hold me, and take me away from dis pain that I feel deep within my soul. I need you. I need you so, so bad, baby. I feel so dirty."

Mudman shook his head. He stood up and picked her up. She wrapped her legs around him. He carried her into the bathroom and cut on the tub after stopping it up. "I'ma wash you up, baby. I'm finna get my baby clean. I promise you." He held her the entire time until the water filled up. Once it filled halfway, he took her clothes from her and lowered her into the water.

Keisha began to shake. She winced in pain as the water irritated the wounds between her thighs and all over her wrists.

She stared up at Mudman as if she were lost. "Please heal me, Mudman. Please, baby. I need you."

Mudman's eyes focused in on her baby bump. It looked so special to him. It gave him the strength and determination to do what he needed to do. "I got you, boo, I swear I will never fail you again. I love you, and I'm finna be every man that you need me to be." He lathered up the loofah and began to wash her delicate body.

Keisha closed her eyes. "He said that he refused to allow for us to be a family. He said that he'd rather die first. He gon' keep coming, Mudman. Prentice gon' keep coming until we kill him, or he kills the both of us. I don't know what I would do if anything happened to you."

"You gotta keep living your life, baby. You gotta keep fight to make your way out of these trenches. Refuse to lose. Make my death mean something. You hear me?"

Keisha shook her head in anger. "No! I'm not finna be in dis world if you ain't in it. I need you, Mudman. We been through way too much together. If you left me alone, I would be so fucked up that I wouldn't know what to do." She jumped back in pain.

Mudman had rubbed the loofah up against her mound. "Damn, boo, I'm sorry. I ain't mean to hurt you."

Keisha nodded. She squeezed her eyelids tighter. "Go ahead, just be gentle."

Mudman opened her lips and proceeded to cleanse her as best he could amidst her wincing and holding his wrist to guide him. After he cleansed her as best he could, she stood up whole he dried her off. Then he picked her up and carried her into the bedroom, where he rubbed her body down with her scented lotions.

After he got her nice and fresh, he climbed into bed behind her and hugged up to her frame. "Come here, baby girl."

Keisha scooted backward until her back side was in his lap. She felt him wrap her within his embrace. He kissed the back of her neck. She smiled and turned all the way around until she was facing him. She held the side of his face. He smelled like Gucci cologne. "Baby, are you getting tired of being with me?"

Mudman was taken off guard. "What?"

Keisha placed her finger on his lips to shush him. "I know that after men have been with a female for an extended period of time that they get sick of the same pussy, and their eyes begin to wander. Is that the case with you and me? Be honest with me." She removed her finger from his lips.

Mudman looked into her pretty brown eyes. "I got curious, baby. I found myself thinking about what it would be like to fuck this particular li'l bitch, and once my mind started to wander, so did my actions. Never once did I stop loving you, or deliberately want to shit on you. I was just curious. I really don't know how to explain it better than that."

Keisha continued to rub his face. "Was she pretty?"

"Seriously, baby, you asking me dat?"

Keisha nodded. "I just wanna know."

"Yeah, she was alright."

"Was she dark-skinned like me? Or did you do like most niggas do when they get a substantial amount of money, go and get yourself a red bone?"

Mudman felt like shit. "She was light-skinned."

"Pretty eyes? What color were her eyes?"

"Keisha? Come on now." He was getting irritated.

"I have a right to know. What color were they?"

He exhaled loudly. "They were green. Now can we please get some sleep? You ain't never gotta worry about that shit ever happening again."

Keisha kissed his lips. "Okay, baby. I believe you."

That night, Keisha couldn't sleep. She stayed awake with her mind racing a million miles a second. She didn't know how to feel inside. She didn't know how she would be rid of the hurt inside of her. All she knew was that she had to get even. She was scorned.

Chapter 13

Mudman carried the baseball bat along the row of bound jack boys that his crew had captured. He was done playing. He'd spent two days laid up with Keisha, trying his best to console her, which meant that he was two days behind on getting The Bull his cash. The five jack boys before him were known for hunting trap houses in his district. They were said to be fearless. He didn't give a fuck about their reputations. All Mudman wanted was his product back so he could hit the ground running again.

He stopped in front of what he told was the head jack boy. He held out the bat and placed the tip against his forehead. "Bitch nigga, you finna tell me where all my product that was taken out of my projects, or yo' homeboys finna watch me make a mess down hurr," he promised. He signaled for Mars to pull the jack boys' chair directly in the middle of the other four chairs so he could be on display. Mudman ripped the duct tape off of his mouth. "Speak, nigga, where is my shit at?"

The dark-skinned jacker mugged Mudman and curled his lip. "Who da fuck is you, cuz? You just came out of nowhere. Don't nobody honor you around Cokeland. Fuck yo' projects. Dese bitches belong to my big homie Nike, not you."

Mudman turned his head to the side and had to seriously look at the young jacker that couldn't be any older than fifteen. "Dat's yo' answer, li'l nigga?"

"Nigga, you lucky you got dat. Now let me go fo' my niggas find out you done made the biggest mistake of yo' life."

Mudman had the apartment packed with his workers. They were bunched in as best as they could be. He looked across all of their faces, including Ashley's, and felt his blood pressure rise. When it came to be a part of the deadly Game of the streets, you couldn't show any weaknesses. Mudman knew

that. Whatever he did at this juncture would define how hard his hittas went for him after Nike was released. He sensed that some of them might have been wavering in their decision to remain loyal to him or to return back to their old hood boss, Nike. "So dat's yo' final answer?"

"Less you want me to call you a bitch-ass nigga in front of all yo' people." He started to crack up. "Free Nike, man, get rid of dis clown." He closed his eyes, laughing. He knew Mudman wasn't going to have the guts to hurt him in a room full of witnesses. She he laughed hard. When he finally opened his eyes, he saw the wooden Louisville Slugger bat coming full speed. It crashed into his forehead, splitting him wide open. He felt so much pain that he farted and screeched.

Mudman wound the bat back again and swung as hard as he could. He cracked the jacker in the temple. The bat dented it in. The jacker began to shake in the chair. Mudman beat his head senseless. He smashed it in until it looked like a ruined jack-o-lantern. The he took a step back and held the bat out. "Who next?" Blood dripped off the tip of it.

He looked into the eyes of the other jack boys. He could see the fear in them. He imagined that they didn't want to happen to them what had just happened to their comrade. "Who next?"

Mars pulled a high yellow jacker's chair in the middle of the living room. "Dis ma'fucka right here known for running up in projects and hitting traps. He was his right hand man, and I got word they he knows what happened to our shit." Mars ripped the tape off of his mouth.

Mudman stepped in front of him. "Speak, nigga. Where my shit at?"

The jack boy looked over to his guy. He had a heavy heart for him. He couldn't believe that anybody would do his homie

like that. "Why da fuck you do my nigga like dat.? He was just a kid, nigga. You don't even know if he - "

CRACK!

Mudman swung the bat with all of his might. It landed on the bridge of the high yellow dude's nose and broke it. Pieces of his bone shot up into his sinuses. He inhaled and felt like he'd breathed in a bunch of knives. Crack! The bat shattered his cranium, and then Mudman was beating him like a maniac, over and over again. He was tired of playing around. Time was of the essence. He sidestepped from beating one jack boy to death to the next. He gave out all head shots. He swung the bat over and over, imagining that each man was Prentice. By the time he finished, he had killed all five of them and was sweating like crazy. The living room looked like a pot of spaghetti had exploded. Fragments of meat and skin littered the carpet along with blood and mucus.

Mudman tossed the bat to Mars. "Get rid of dat ma'fucka, and get rid of dese bodies. As soon as dis mess is cleaned up, we finna pull our own series of kick doors until we get dis money back. Everybody understand that?" He looked around the room at nodding heads. His phone vibrated. He saw that it was Miguelito's number. He ignored it and replaced the phone. He had two hundred thousand dollars put up. He was five hundred and twenty thousand short. He had two traps that he'd just dropped off four kilos a piece. He was banking on their success, but even if things went the way they were supposed to, he would still be short when it was all said and done.

Mars came and rested his hand on his shoulder. "Boss, we got a problem." He had his phone to his ear.

Mudman frowned. "What's da problem?"

"Nike just got out. A bunch of niggas from Crenshaw just went and picked him up. My informant say they were like ten cars deep."

"Crenshaw? Who da fuck do he know out there?" Mudman wanted to know.

Mars shrugged his shoulders. "I don't know for sure, but I do know that he grew up over in Crenshaw, and he didn't move out here to Cokeland until he was about fourteen. That's when he plugged in with them Acorn hittas before they got indicted. That nigga got a few plugs all over California. I still don't know how he beat all dat shit he was charged with, but it is what it is. He wanna have a sit down wit' you right away. Are you up to it?"

"A sit down? Are you fuckin' kidding me? What the fuck he wanna have a sit down wit' me for?"

"He wants his streets back. Dat nigga say he ready to die fo' dat shit," Mars relayed.

Mudman eyed him with anger. "Is dat right?"

"Yeah, dat's what was told to me."

"A'ight den. You tell homeboy I'll meet his ass tonight. We can nip dis shit in the bud right away."

"Will do." Mars walked off with his phone to his ear.

Ashley waited until he stepped away before she approached Mudman. She stepped in front of him and leaned in. "Hey Mudman, you alright? You seem stressed out?"

He nodded. "Yeah, it's just too much shit going on. My brain ain't getting a second to think right before somethin else happens."

"I can understand that." She looked both ways and noticed that a few of the workers were watching them. She lowered her voice as low as she could. "Daddy, I missed you. I been thinking about you every second of every day. I think I'm going crazy. Do you think that maybe we can spend some time together soon?"

Mudman rubbed his temples in a circular motion. "Seriously, Ashley, I can't even think straight right now. I got so

much shit going on that I can't see that shit happening no time soon."

"No time soon? What is dat supposed to mean?" she asked, looking around at the nosy bystanders that were eyeing them.

"Dat means that we over wit', shawty. I gotta concentrate on my streets and hold Keisha down more than I been doing. Dat's my baby. I should have never been fuckin' wit' you on dat level no way." He brushed past her and entered back into the living film.

Ashley felt like her heart had been ripped out of her chest. She eased past the crowd and into the hallway. Her tears began to fall. Before she could make it into the bathroom, Mars was coming out of it. They nearly bumped into each other. She tried to hide her face.

Mars grabbed her. "Ashley, what's the matter with you?"

"Nothin'," she lied. "I'm just going through somethin' right now. I'll be okay." She pulled her arm from him and closed the bathroom door.

Mars listened outside of it for a second. He could hear her break all the way down. She sounded like she was being ripped in two. He was listening by the door when Mudman stepped into the hallway. He straightened up. "Dawg, you know what's the matter wit' Ashley? She crying in da bathroom right now." He pointed toward the bathroom with his thumb.

"Just ended shit wit' her. Dat's probably what it is. She'll be a'ight doe. I'ma fuck wit' her later. Come on, I need you to give me the low down on dis Nike nigga." Mudman led him out of the hallway.

Mars kept looking back over his shoulders. He wanted to go back and console Ashley. Though they weren't on the same

page, she was still his baby mother. That meant that it was his job to protect her. "A'ight, bruh, what you wanna know?"

That night it stormed like crazy. Rain coursed across the sky, carried by harsh winds. Lightning flashed every few minutes. Its Kodak-like electricity was followed by the roar of thunder. Mudman pushed his Porsche truck through the harsh conditions with his Tech on his lap. He had the windshield wipers on high. A bulletproof vest was latched tightly around his chest and midsection.

"Man, I still think you crazy ass a muthafucka to be rolling to Los Angeles to see dis nigga. You should have made him bring his ass to Oakland. Dat's where you running shit at. For all we know, this fool finna bum rush us and chop our bodies into little bitty pieces."

Mudman smirked. "A scared man is a dead man. Fuck dis nigga. I ain't afraid to go. If it's my time, it's my time. That's all it is to dat shit right dere."

"Dat's selfish doe, bruh. What about Keisha? What about yo' twins? You can't be taking dese suicidal-ass missions like dis. Who da fuck gon' hold yo' people down if you get smoked?"

Mudman shrugged his shoulders. "Den I guess it'll be in my best interest to not get smoked den." He smiled at Mars and turned up his codeine bottled water. He felt murderous.

"I guess you right." Mars still felt like they were making the wrong decision, but seeing as how Mudman was dead set on doing whatever he wanted to do, he felt like he didn't have any other choice but to see things through. "I got a chance to have a few words with Ashley. She fucked up over you." Mars hated admitting that.

"She'll be awright. I told her up in the beginning that I would never fuck off Keisha. We wasn't never supposed to cross dat line to begin wit'. But it is what it is. Dat shit ain't important." He pulled into the parking lot of the boxing gym where they were set to meet Nike. He parked next to two trucks after turning his car around so that the front end would be facing the exit of the parking space. He cut the engine. "You ready?"

Mars nodded. "'Bout as ready as I'll ever be." Mars watched their troops park all over the parking lot. They hopped out of their vans and stood in the rain on point, per Mudman's orders.

Mudman smiled at his killas. He opened the door to his truck, and then closed it back. The rain bead down on his head. He tucked both of his pistols and carried the Tech .9 in his hand. He beat on the door to the gym.

A few moments later, the door was opened. A big body-guard looked down on him. He had the Tech .9 resting up against his shoulder. "Dat nigga Nike wanna see me, mane. Tell homeboy I'm hurr and ready for dis sit-down thang."

The bodyguard nodded and opened the door. "Step on in."

Mudman stepped past him and into the gym. He looked ahead and saw that the gym was in complete darkness with the exception of the light shining on the boxing ring. Around the ring were twenty killas. All of them had blue bandannas around their faces.

Nike stood up. "Mudman, come up here and fuck wit' a nigga. What it do, cuz?"

Mudman stepped up to the ring and ducked under the ropes. He saw that the ring had a long table set up in the center of it. The table was covered with all kinds of food and drinks. Mudman walked right up to the table and flipped it with one hand. He mugged Nike and got into his face. "Nigga, I'm from

115

Baton Rouge, boy, we don't do no ma'fuckin' sit downs with rivals. We stand on our two feet until a ma'fucka knock us up off dem bitches."

Nike stood six feet even. He was 220 pounds of solid muscle, bald, with a Muslim-like beard. "Well, nigga, I'm from California, and out here we give a ma'fucka a chance to get they mind right before we knock dat bitch off dey shoulders. Dis yo' final chance to get an understanding wit' me, Loc. It's in yo' best interest, or shit finna get real ugly." He held out his arms. His troops cocked their weapons and stepped closer to the stage.

Mudman didn't flinch. "Cokeland is mine. I ain't sharing it wit' no nigga. Ma'fucka ain't taking shit from me either. Bitch nigga, you can get it in blood if you want it." Mudman pressed the Tech up under Nike's chin. "Fuck you wanna do?"

Mars cursed under his breath. "Fuck." He pulled his gat out of the small of his back and looked around.

Nike's troops climbed into the ring, aiming their guns at Mudman and Mars. There were so many beams on Mudman that there was no way he would have been able to survive all of those slugs. Mars was sure of it. He didn't even want to pay attention to the ones that were placed on him.

Nike looked into Mudman's eyes. "You sho' you wanna do dis? You kill me, and dey gon' kill you."

"Like I said, bitch nigga, if you want anythang from me, you gon' have to get that shit in blood."

The door to the gym popped open and Miguelito stepped inside with thirty of his Cartel Killas. He tossed a grenade up and down in his hand. "Boys, boys, boys. Come on now. It's impossible to war and make money, and that's all that we care about down in Sinaloa, that you make some fuckin' money!" he spat. He climbed into the ring and faced Mudman. "You been ignoring me."

Mudman dismissed him quickly. "I ain't tryna hear dat shit. Dis nigga thank he 'bout to get anythang from me, he got another muthafuckin' thang coming."

Miguelito stepped up and placed his hand on Nike's shoulder. "I'm sure we can find a way to make dis work."

Hood Rich

Chapter 14

Mudman went on a rampage after the meeting between Nike and Miguelito. They had come to an agreement that Nike would stay far away from Oakland until Mudman was given the opportunity to make back what he owed The Bull and the original Bull Thirsty Cartel. Mudman felt he didn't need Miguelito to step in and make peace. He was on some radical, no mercy shit. He sent his troops to kick in doors and raid trap houses all over Oakland. If they weren't under his regime, they were fair game. He placed Mars in a position of absolute power and control. He supplied him with ten killas that were ordered by Mudman to do everything that he said. Mars had plans on using that to his advantage.

Mudman refused to sit back while his army of killas flooded the streets. He kicked in doors as well and laid rival dope boys on their stomachs. He cleaned out their stashes and took pride in knocking the backs of their heads off if they refused to give up the goods. Mudman wasn't playing no games. He was getting it in blood.

Keisha was worried about him. He was displaying behaviors that she had never seen before. His temper was shorter. He tended to do more dope than she had ever witnessed him do before. On the third day after the meeting, she found Mudman laid out on the couch snoring with a Draco on his lap and a .9 millimeter in his left hand. She stood watching him for a short while. He mumbled under his breath and frowned, then continued to snore. He seemed to be squeezing his eyelids harder and harder. Keisha found this odd.

She slowly made her way over to him. When she got four steps away, Mudman's upped the Draco and pointed the .9 at her with his eyes still closed. "Move another fuckin' step and I'll blow yo' muthafuckin head off. Fuck you thank dis is?"

Keisha was stunned. She bucked her eyes. "Baby, what are you talking about?"

Mudman slowly opened his eyes. They were glossy. His pupils were dilated. Keisha's face was blurry at first. Then it came into view. He perked up, and sat up straight on the couch. "Shit. Fuck. My fault, baby. I'm bugging."

Keisha was shaking. She looked at the table and saw that it was covered with stacks of money on one side. On the other was a plate full of heroin. A razorblade lay smack dab in the middle of it, alongside of a rolled up hundred dollar bill. Keisha winced. "Mudman, how much of that stuff have you done?" She was concerned for his well-being.

Mudman nodded and began to snore loudly. His head fell forward until it wound up the in his lap. Then he jerked awake and aimed both guns at her again. "What's wrong wit' you?' He hollered.

Keisha jumped back. "Baby, it's me." She held up her hands and continued to walk up on him.

Mudman blinked his eyes a bunch of times. Then he bucked them wide open. He lowered his weapons and jumped up. He rushed to the window of the townhouse they were renting and looked out of it. "They coming, Keisha. I almost got enough money, but dey wanna see me fail anyway. Dey wanna see me fail, baby. I'm trying. Lord knows I'm trying!" he hollered.

Keisha placed both of her hands on her face. She was so worried that she didn't know what to do. "Who's coming, baby? Talk to me."

"The Bull, Prentice, all of dem. The cartels. I fucked over a lot of cartels. They all wanna see me bleed. But I'm a mutha-fuckin' souljah. They can't kill me. I stand as a man on my own two feet. You can't kill a muthafucka that's already dead!" he yelled, peeking out of the window. He placed the

curtain back in place after seeing his hittas roaming around his pad on security.

"Mudman, I thank we should just leave. We need to get as far away from California, and dese cartels, as possible. We ain't got shit to prove. We can take dat money right dere and live good for a while. Come on, baby. Please listen to me."

"And let dem win? Are you fuckin' serious? I'd rather die first." He placed his Draco on the couch and pulled Keisha to him. "Shawty, you don't believe in me no mo'? Huh? Dat it? You thank dese niggas better than me? Huh? You thank dey can kill us? After all we fuckin' been through?" He held her arm tighter and tighter.

Keisha slapped his face and pushed him away from her. "Get the fuck off of me, nigga. I don't know what yo' problem is, but you better get yo' shit together."

Mudman stumbled backwards and laughed. "Damn, dat's how you feel?" He sat on the couch and created two thick limes of Tar. He placed the rolled-up dollar bill into his left nostril and snorted it as hard as he could. Then, before he even picked his head up, he placed the bill into his right nostril and tooted up the second line. The drug hit his brain and sent chill bumps all over his skin. His heart slowed all the way down. His vision got blurry. He felt tense, then all of a sudden his heart started to beat so fast that he felt like he couldn't breathe. He stood up and fell to his knees. "Keisha! Shit!" He clutched his chest and fell to the floor.

Keisha hurried to his side and knelt down beside him. "Rome! Baby, what's the matter?" she screamed.

Mudman's vision went in and out. It felt like an elephant was sitting on his chest. He struggled to get up, but he couldn't move. He closed his eyes tight. When he opened them again, the entire room looked as if it was a sea of red. He closed them back.

Keisha ran out of the room and came back with a pitcher of ice water. She poured it slowly on his face, then grabbed his head and squirted Narcan up his nose.

Mudman jumped before he shook uncontrollably. He choked on his own spit and rolled on his side, shaking.

Keisha jumped up and began to panic. "Fight, baby! Fight! Please fight!"

Mudman could hear her though her voice sounded like a million echoes were coming out of it. He opened his eyes and located her. He had double vision. His insides felt like they were trying to come out of his nose. His ribs seemed as if they were being crushed by an eighteen wheeler. He curled into a ball and reached out for Keisha.

Keisha fell to her knees and crawled over to him. She felt his shaking body and tried to hug him. "I got you, boo. I got you. I ain't going nowhere. It's me, and you," she assured him.

The effects of the Narcan began to reverse the overdose that threatened to take over him. His shaking subsided. He eased from a ball to lying flat out on his back. A trickle of blood seeped from both nostrils.

Keisha wiped it away with her thumbs. She slid into his embrace and hugged up to him more firmly. "You okay, baby? Please tell me you are."

Mudman felt like shit. His head was pounding like an eight oh eight drum. He wanted to throw up. He fought the bile trying to rise from his belly. "I'm sick, baby. I feel like I got a fever. I'm scorching. I need you to get me into the tub. Fill it up with as much ice as you can find. Please."

Keisha ran out of the room to follow his orders. She turned the cold water on the tub. Then she ran back and forth, dumping ice into it. When she emptied out the deep freezer with all of the ice that they had stored up, she helped Mudman to strip off all of his clothes, then guided him into the tub slowly.

Mudman sank inside of it. He began shaking again. He lowered himself until the water came to his neck. Then he closed his eyes. "I love you, Keisha. I swear I never knew what love was until I feel knee deep in it wit' you."

Keisha got down on her knees and dipped the towel into the tub. Then she ran the towel all over his body. She wrung it out over the top of his head to help to bring his body temperature down. "Mudman, you are the love of my life. I thank I always been in love wit' you even when I wasn't supposed to have been. There has always thing pulling of myself to you, even when I was with Prentice."

Mudman's entire body was aching worse than he ever remember it aching before. He smiled and tried to ignore the feeling of being stabbed over and over that was taking place in his stomach. "I didn't care if you and Prentice were happy, Keisha. No matter what, I was always going to come for you. You held me down in Angola when nobody else wanted to step up the plate. You did. Dem ma'fuckas told me dey wasn't gon' feed us in dere, baby, unless we worked dey fields like we was slaves a something. But I told 'em to kiss my ass. I had enough commissary to last me because you made sure I was straight as much as you could. You ain't have to do dat, shawty, but you did. For dat reason, I'ma die trying to give you the world." He hugged his right arm across his ribs.

Keisha felt emotional. She loved Mudman so much. Sometimes it pained her how much. "Baby, being there for you was no problem. It's sickening how they do y'all in Angola. They got y'all working da fields while they ride around on horses. It's too reminiscent of the slavery days of the past. I'm sorry that you had to go through that."

Mudman cringed and hopped out of the tub. Water splashed everywhere. The sounds of his wet feet hitting the

floor resonated in the bathroom. He pulled up the lid to the toilet and stuck his head inside of it, puking his guts.

Keisha rubbed his back. "Honey, do you thank we should go to the hospital?"

Mudman continued to puke. His stomach tightened so bad that it felt like it was about to burst each time he cringed. After he threw up as much as he felt he could, he sat back on his haunches and closed the toilet. He flushed it and wiped his mouth with the back of his hand. He felt cold.

Keisha hugged him. "Should we go, baby?"

Mudman shivered. "We can't. I'm wanted all over the country now, shawty. Ma'fuckas see my face, they gon' turn me in. We can't trust it." He hugged her body. "I'ma beat dis shit. Dis shit ain't about to break me." He wiped his mouth again and started to stand up.

Keisha got to her feet before him. She helped him come to his. "Be careful, baby. Please. Come on, let me lead you back to the bedroom so you can lay down." She wrapped her arm around his waist and guided him.

Mudman was dizzy. His head felt like it was spinning worse than ever. He felt nauseous. He threw up in the back of his throat and swallowed it. He continued to lean against Keisha.

When they got to the room, Keisha helped him to get into the bed. She pulled back the blankets. When he got under them, she pulled them back over him.

"Baby, I thank we need some sort of doctor right now. Something could be seriously wrong wit' you."

Mudman squeezed his eyelids together. "Nall, shawty, I just tooted too much of dat shit. I'll be a'ight. I just need to lay here for a minute. Get yo' ass up here and straddle me," he ordered.

Keisha was taken off guard by his request. "You sho'? Ain't you hurting right now?"

Mudman nodded. "Yeah, but so what? I need to feel my strength on top of me. Get up here."

Keisha kicked off her house shoes and climbed on top of him. She was as careful as she could be. When she was properly situated, she laid her head on his chest. She could smell each breath that he took. If it were anybody else's vomit-smelling breath it would have turned her stomach, but since it was Mudman, she took delight in his sense. She didn't care how weird that made her seem. She held his face, and kissed his neck. "I love you, Rome."

He placed both of his hands on her backside. "I love you too. I need you to know that we are in some heavy shit, but I'ma find a way to get us up out of dis. I'ma get dat nigga Prentice back too. He'll never get away with what he did to you."

Keisha smiled. "I know you are. There is no doubt in my mind that you're going to make him pay, but how about if you didn't?"

Mudman was shocked. "What?"

"Well, baby, I been reading the Word a lot lately, and in the Bible of says that revenge is mine says the Lord. So it's not for us to get him back. God will get him back in His own time."

Mudman shook his head. "Shawty, I don't know what you talking 'bout, but yo' man is the Reaper. When it's time for ma'fuckas to get snatched off of this earth, I am the one that God sends to crush dey ass. Matter fact, the only time he allow for ma'fuckas like Prentice to get dealt with is when he sends a ma'fucka like me. Dat nigga gon' get da bidness. I can't see it no other way."

Hood Rich

Keisha nodded. "Well, you're the man, and I just follow you. But I just feel it deep in my heart that we need to leave California. We need to get as far away from here as we possibly can."

"I can agree wit' you on dat. But first, I gotta close all of these loose ends. After I put out the fires that I started, we'll be ready to go. But I don't wanna thank about dat right now. Come on, let's get some shut eye." He hugged her closer to his body and nodded out.

Keisha laid on top of him for a long time before she began to pray for their forgiveness. Her heart felt heavy by their sins. She was tired of carrying the load. She simply wanted them to get right with God. She wanted to leave their sinful pasts behind. She wanted for them to have new beginnings before their children came into the world. She prayed that they weren't in too deep. She prayed that there was still time.

Chapter 15

"What you say you got again over dere?" Mudman asked Mars.

Mars was sitting in front of a pile of cash on the floor. He had counted the money three times and had come up with the same total. He didn't understand why Mudman didn't use money counting machines like everybody else in the twenty-first century? "Bruh, the same total as before. Dis is four hundred and fifty thousand dollars on the head. If we used money counters, it would tell you da same thang."

"Nigga, I ain't ask yo' black ass all dat. Four hundred and fifty thousand dollars was all I needed to know. Dat's good. Now what you come up with over dere, shawty?"

Ashley pushed her stacks in front of her. She was the only one sitting at the wooden round table. "I got two hundred and fifty thousand right here. I counted it three times, bill for bill, and that's what it keep coming to."

"A'ight, that's seven hundred thousand all together. I got five hundred in front of me. Two of it goes to The Bull, and the other three is for our business. We made it in time. Dat's what the fuck I'm talking 'bout right dere." He clapped his hands together and stood up. "Mars, you pick out two of your closest security detail. I'm having you jump on interstate 5 tonight. You taking this money personally to The Bull. Can you handle dat?"

Mars looked him over from the corners of his eyes. "You already know dat I can."

"A'ight, cool. When you get back, we gon' celebrate the fact that I am officially making you my right hand man. Ma'fuckas are to honor you as a king. When they don't see me, you are the head. And when they see us together, they are to honor you like dey honor me. How dat sound to you?"

Mars put on a fake smile. He could never get excited about being under no man. As far as he was concerned, he was the king. Mudman's time was coming to a close. He was going to make sure of that. Though his patience was wearing thin, he knew that patience was the key rule in the game. He who had the most patience was able to analyze the other player's mistakes and capitalize off of them. He stood up and shook up with Mudman. They embraced.

"Dawg, I love you, nigga. You hear me? I'm glad that we figured dis shit out. Now that we have, we should be able to fully conquer dis city and start to venture over to both San Francisco and Los Angeles."

Mudman stepped back. "Dat sounds like a plan. But first thang first, you go 'head and get your security detail in order. I'ma call The Bull and Miguelito and get your party ready. Da Projects finna be lit tonight." He punched his fist into the palm of his hand.

Mars nodded. "A'ight, I'll fuck wit you in a minute. Come on, Ashley."

Ashley shook her head. "I'm cool, Mars, I need to holler at Mudman for a minute. I'll hit you up in a minute."

Mars was taken aback. He thought they were moving forward now that she and Mudman were no longer messing around. "You sho'?"

She nodded. "Yeah."

Mars came over and stood in front of her chair. "A'ight, well give me a hug den. I mean, we still good, right?"

Ashley glanced over at Mudman. She blushed. She didn't know if he knew that she and Mars were back talking or what. She hated that Mars had to be so fuckin' needy. She stood up, and gave him a petty ass hug. She needed him to leave already.

Mars felt her cold embrace and grew envious of Mudman again. He knew that Ashley was acting funny because he was

in the room. He hated Mudman, especially because of how Ashley was acting. He was a sucka for her. She only settled for him out of necessity for their daughter. He broke the embrace and smiled. "A'ight. I'ma get dis shit together and be at you in a second, Mudman."

"Nigga, quit saying you finna leave and bounce already. Damn. Time is money. I ain't finna move in on yo' li'l bitch. Me and Keisha straight." He laughed.

Ashley blushed. "I am my own woman. Don't nobody own me."

Mars frowned. "What?"

"You heard me," she insisted.

Mudman smacked his lips. He stepped into her face. "So you saying you wouldn't belong to me if I wanted you to?" He looked into her green eyes with his gray ones.

Ashley felt weak and mesmerized. She held her silence. She didn't understand how Mudman could have such a control over her, how he could make her putty with just his presence, but he had that way about himself. She was stuck looking into his eyes.

Mars had seen all he could handle. "A'ight den." His mind was officially made up. He was going to fuck Mudman over. Mudman had given him no choice.

As soon as the door closed behind Mars, Mudman busted up laughing and pulled Ashley to him. He kissed her on the cheek. "Come on, shawty, and help me throw all of dis money in a bag. I gotta package it so Mars can move it tonight."

"Mudman, I'm pregnant," Ashley blurted out.

Mudman was smiling. His face went blank as soon as the words spilled out of her mouth. He released her and stood back to look over her shoulders. "What you say?"

Ashley backed up and took a seat at the table in front of her piles of money. "I'm pregnant with your kid. I know

you're not going to want me to keep it, but I am. I am because I don't believe in dat abortion shit, and because I love you."

Mudman ran his fingers through his long dreads. "Nall, shawty, you tripping. You can't keep my seed. Keisha gon' kill my ass, and yours. Fuck is you thanking?" he snapped. He grabbed three thousand dollars and tried to hand it to her.

Ashley glared at him with mounting anger. "Didn't you hear a word of what I just said? Huh?"

Mudman frowned. "Bitch, I heard what you said, but I'm telling you that you ain't got dat option. You gotta get rid of it. If I'ma have a child in dis world, I'ma be there for my seed every single day. I'ma be faithful to its mother, and it will never see its mother hurting because of me. I will be fully devoted to both her and my child."

"Mudman. I. Am. Not. Having. An. Abortion. Get. Dat. Shit. Through. Your. Big. Ass. Head. Now, did I say it slow enough for you, or you need me to say it slower den dat?"

Mudman mugged her for a second. Then he grabbed her by her hair and pulled her to him. His forehead rested against hers. "Shawty, who da fuck you thank you talking to like dat?"

"My muthafuckin daddy. Now what? Nigga, I love yo' ass. You my daddy. I'm having dis baby. And whenever shit fuck up between you and Keisha, you gon' brang yo' ass back to me, and we gon' live happily ever after. We are meant to be together. I know it, and I don't give a damn if you do or not." She held her still face. "So what you gon' do now? You gon' rip my hair out of my scalp. You gon' beat me? You gon' kill me? Huh, daddy?"

Mudman continued to eye her. He didn't know what to say or do. Ultimately it was her choice to bear their child or to not have it. He only wished he could help her to see things his way. He released her and slightly nudged her backward. "Shawty, what da fuck is it about me dat make you wanna be

wit' me so bad? Huh? I don't treat you da greatest. I do me, and when I fuck that pussy, I don't be making love to dat shit. I beat dat bitch in like a savage cause dat's just who I am. So what is it?"

She fixed her hair and shrugged her shoulders. "I don't know, and I ain't gotta explain myself to you. I'm having dis baby. I'm in love wit' you, and I'ma be here for a long time unless you kill me." She sat down and crossed her thighs.

"So what's dis shit wit' you and Mars?" he questioned. He didn't give a fuck that they were messing around, but he needed to know the possibilities of Mars being the father of the child.

"We talking. No fuckin' though. We ain't did dat in two years. And never will again. I don't get down like dat. I just want him to take care of his daughter. Dat's all, or go the fuck away because dat works for me too." She licked her juicy lips. "So what we gon' do?"

Mudman sat on the couch. "I gotta tell Keisha to see what she say. I already know she finna snap. But I gotta keep shit one hunnit wit' her."

Ashley stood up. "Nall, let me do it. After all, we was fuckin' around behind her back. I should be woman enough to let her know what's really good."

Mudman shook his head. "Damn, it seem like every time I figure out on thing a bunch of other shit become unraveled. And you telling me dat you not budging on dis abortion thing?"

"In fact, if you ask me about it again, I'ma make you whoop my ass. Now the answer is no. Dat's just that."

Mudman sighed. "Den dat's what it is den. I'ma do my part. You ain't finna have to worry about shit. Ain't no dead beat in me. You should already know that."

"I do. But still, I wanna be the one to sit down with Keisha and tell her what's good. Grant me that."

"You can. Just be prepared to go to war," he said.

"Oh, I am."

Mars took his ear away from the door, and swung at the air. He was so mad after hearing Mudman, and Ashley's conversation that he felt like killing something. He nodded his head and made his way out of the hallway of the building. After jumping in his Lexus truck, he texted Nike to let him know that he was on his way to their usual meeting place. They had to come up with a plan to get rid of Mudman once and for all.

Figgady was sitting at the counter eating a sandwich when Linda came into the kitchen with a bottle of Hennessey in her hand. She drank directly from it. She had on a short robe. The belt hung loosely around her waist. It threatened to open. He watched her throat move up and down.

"Damn, Linda, you okay?" he asked with a mouthful of food.

She took her mouth away from the bottle. "How can I be, Figgady, when I know my man the one dat did dis shit to my sister?" she slurred. She took another long swallow from the bottle. Her robe opened enough to show him her left breast. The brown nipple looked huge, just like Lainey's had been. He figured that big nipples must run in her family.

"What you mean? You thank Pooty did dat to Lainey?"

"Yep. I heard him in dere telling you how much he used to lust after my baby sister. It got me sick as hell just hearing

da words come out of his mouth. Now he up dere all asleep like everythang is cool. I swear to God, I wanna kill his ass," she snapped. "Dat duffel bag of money he got don't mean shit to me."

Figgady's ears perked up. "What you talking 'bout?"

She took another swallow. She pointed upstairs. "He got a black duffel bag full of money up dere. Say he gotta go purchase some dope from the Mexicans or some shit. I don't know. All I do know is dat he gon' have to pay for what he did to Lainey." She pulled a butcher's knife out of the knife holder. "Been building up the nerve all week to do dis. Now I'm ready."

Figgady mugged her, and then smiled. It was getting boring being around Pooty and Linda all day. The house had taken on a somber ambiance now that Lainey had been killed. He was tired of the both of them. He felt it would be peaceful to have the house to himself while he hunted Prentice.

He got up and stepped over to the drunken Linda. He slid his arm around her neck. "Look, come here. Let me tell you something that you gotta keep between us. From his viewpoint, he could see her big nipple even better. It looked suckable. The Percocets had him feeling hornier than a pervert on Viagra.

Linda looked up to him. "What you gotta tell me?"

Figgady led her to the living room. All he could think about was the bag of money she spoke of. "Look, I love my cousin. But he did admit to fucking yo' li'l sister a lot. When she wanted to tell you 'cause she ain't wanna do it no more, he snapped. And, well... you already know da rest."

Linda's tears were already falling down her cheeks. "How could he do dis? How?" she cried. She clutched the knife harder in her hand and jerked from under Figgady's shoulder.

"I'm finna kill him. I'm finna kill him for what he did to Lainey!" she hollered, making her way up the stairs.

Chapter 16

Figgady stepped into the room behind Linda. She held the butcher's knife in her hand. She crept over to the bed where Pooty was snoring like a bear. She stood crying for a full minute. All of the good memories that she'd had with him flashed through her mind. It nearly caused her to second guess what she was about to do. But then she saw Lainey's book bag hanging up on the door knob of her bedroom closet. She grew angry. She raised the knife in the sky. "I hate you! How could you do that to Lainey?"

Pooty stopped snoring. His eyes popped open just as the blade came crushing through his Adam's apple. It sliced through his throat and poked the back of his neck. Blood spurted across the sheets. He jumped up with the knife sticking out of his neck, his eyes big as pool balls.

"Oh my God! Oh my God! What have I done? What have I done?"

Pooty staggered backward and crashed his back into the wall. Figgady could hear him gurgling on his own blood. Pooty eyed his cousin in the doorway eating a sandwich as if it was the most natural thing in the world. He reached out for him. He needed his help. His back landed against the wall. He slid down it. It felt like the knife was ripping the insides of his throat out. It was the worst pain he'd ever felt in his entire life.

Figgady finished the sandwich. "She say you killed her sister. I told her how you used to fuck li'l shawty all the time." Figgady laughed. He walked over and grabbed the duffel bag full of cash that was on the side of the bed. He unzipped it and looked inside. He pulled out a ten thousand dollar stack. He thumbed through the bills and nodded his head. "I guess money is thicker than blood, huh?"

Linda was freaking out. She didn't know what. "Help him, Figgady. Help him. Oh my God, what have I done?"

Pooty kicked his legs. He began to shake. Blood spurted out of the middle of his neck like a leaky pipe. Every time he moved, it sank deeper into his throat.

Figgady zipped up the bag. He grabbed Linda by the hair and pulled her back to him. His lips rested on her right earlobe. "Why you do dat to my cousin? You killed him."

"I know. I know. I know. I'm so sorry. Lord knows I'm so sorry." She began to cry harder.

Figgady knocked her to the floor. Then he got down with her and straddled her body. He pulled her robe wide open and threw the sash over his shoulders. She lay naked before him. Her body looked immaculate. Her nipples were so big that they covered the majority of her mounds. Her stomach had a belly button that came out slightly. It was decorated by a belly ring. Below it was her pussy. Lightly-trimmed. The lips were fat and heavily engorged. It mirrored Lainey's. He sniffed her box. He held her thighs wide open before licking up and down her slit.

She beat at his back. "What is wrong wit' you? Get off of me!" she hollered.

Figgady took the blows. "Dat's what she said." He laughed. He climbed up her body, pulled out his piece, and slammed it home. He proceeded to fuck her like a raging bull.

Pooty's life slowly slipped away from him. The world seemed to get dimmer and dimmer. With his last ounce of strength he took a hold of the handle, and slowly pulled it out of his throat inch by inch. When the final piece of the steel was out, a geyser of blood poured into his chest. He fell forward and died.

Figgady saw him fall over and pounded Linda harder. He flipped her over and got to dogging her from the back at full

speed while she cried and screamed under him. He eyed Lainey's book bag and came deep within her womb. The sight of Lainey's book bag triggered something inside of him that he didn't even know was there.

Linda closed her eyes and continued to grown louder and louder. There was nothing that she could do other than to let Figgady have his way. She had killed his cousin, after all. She was lost. She didn't know what was going to happen after he finished with her.

Mars pulled the black van into the garage and jumped out of it. Nike's men closed the garage door and stood with their backs against it on security. Mars walked up to Nike and shook up with him. "What up, cuz?"

Nike nodded. "You know what it is, Loc. You brought dem presidents?"

"Like it's a muthafuckin' election," Mars jacked. He eased back into the van. "Come sit wit' me for a minute."

Nike jumped into the van and looked around it after Mars activated the interior lights. He saw one duffel bag after the next. "Damn, my nigga. How much bread is dis?"

"Nine hundred thousand. Dis shit belongs to Mudman. I'm supposed to be dropping it off to The Bull down in Sinaloa right now, but we got a change of plans. You and yo' men about to shop dis bitch down and blow dis ma'fuckin' van up. Mudman gon' lose dis money, and The Bull gon' handle his bidness. After dat nigga move out da way, we gon' pay the Bull what Mudman owed him. He gon' plug us into them narcotics, and its gon' be a wrap. I'ma sit on the throne of Oak-

land. You gon' have Los Angeles, and we gone buss San Francisco down the middle. In two years we should be so rich that we don't know what to do."

Nike nodded. "Hell yeah, I like the sound of dat. When we finna do all dis shit?"

"Gotta be tonight. I'm supposed to already be on da road right now."

"A'ight, say no more. You running da show, just tell me what you need me to do."

"A'ight, peep dis..." Mars began, and then he let him know how they were going to pull off one of the biggest double crosses in California history.

Figgady pulled out of Linda. His dick was sore. He had been fucking her for two hours straight in every position that he could think of. He climbed off of her and stood up. "So what you gon' do now, shawty?"

Linda continued to lay on her back with her thighs wide open. Her pussy looked like it had been through a pounding. The lips were slightly parted, enough to expose her bubble gum pink. She covered her face with her hands. A puddle of blood made its way toward her head. "I don't know what to do. I can't go to jail. I don't wanna be in that hellhole for the rest of my life," she cried.

"Then I guess you know yo' only other option huh?" He pulled a .45 from his waist and cocked it. "You gotta take yo'self out the game, shawty."

Linda closed her thighs and stood up. "I'm not strong enough to do dat either."

Figgady lowered the gun. "Den I don't know what else to tell you."

Linda looked down on Pooty. He lay with his eyes wide open. "You did it to her, didn't you?"

"What?"

"It was you that killed my sister all along, wasn't it?" She wiped a tear from her left eye and sniffled.

"Dat's fucked up, ain't it?" He busted up laughing. "Here it is that you done killed a nigga you been in love wit' all dis time, when all along I was the ma'fucka that smoked shawty's ass and tossed her into the garbage can. I'm just saying, you gotta feel like shit." He shook his head.

Linda's heart sank. "Why? Why did you do dis to our family? We were good to you."

"Fuck y'all family. I ain't got one, so why should y'all? Dat shit ain't fair." He looked down on Pooty again. "Plus dat nigga used to whoop my ass when we was little. I always told him when I grew up dat I was gon' get his punk ass back. Well... Got my get back." He started laughing again.

Linda fell to her knees. She was in utter shock and disbelief. "So now what?"

"Now you gotta kill yo'self. Its dat simple."

"I'm not doing dat. What else you got?" she said dejectedly.

"Aw, dat was yo' final option." Figgady pulled a silencer out of his pocket and screwed it on to his .45. "Any last words?"

Linda crawled over to Pooty and hugged up with him. He was coated in blood. She felt lost. She couldn't believe that she had allowed for her alcohol consumption to cause her kill the love of her life. She should have known that he would have never hurt Lainey. Ever since Lainey had been a toddler, he'd treated her as his own little sister. Linda felt so foolish. She snuggled as much under Pooty as she could. She pulled him back by the neck, and rested his face against hers.

Figgady stood back. "Go 'head, get comfortable now. Let me know when you ready."

Linda remained still. "God gon' get you for what you did to dis family."

Figgady laughed. "Yeah, well, your family gotta wait in line cause a ma'fucka destroyed mine first. So when God takes him off da earth, den I'll know dat he working his way around to me." Figgady stood over her. "By da way. You and yo' sister a tie when it comes to da pussy. Both of y'all got good boxes."

"Fuck you!"

BOOF! BOOF! BOOF! BOOF! Figgady fingered his trigger back to back, giving her all facials. He checked her pulse, confirming that she was deceased. He grabbed the duffel bag and bounced out of the front door of their home. He jumped into his Buick Lacrosse and pulled away from the curb.

Prentice waited until he pulled down the block before he pulled off behind him. He kept a short distance. His Tech .9 rested on his lap. "I got yo' ass now, Figgady. How da fuck you thank you big ass ain't gon' stand out in Los Angeles. You distinctive as fuck." He laughed with murder plaguing his mind.

"A'ight, I gotta pull dis ma'fucka over, I gotta piss like a ma'fucka," Mars said, looking over at Ashley.

"Boy, you tripping. You better hold dat shit. Ain't nothin' out here but a bunch of damn farms. You gotta be out of yo' damn mind."

Mars smacked his lips. "Fuck what you talking 'bout. You ain't never been on one dese runs before. Once you get a little further down the state ain't gon' be no more time to piss. You gon' have to hold dat shit. So like I said. I'm finna pull over up here and piss. Fuck what you talking about."

Ashley waved him off. "Do you den." But now that he was talking about using the bathroom, she suddenly felt like she had to go. She looked out into the cornfields that they were passing and got nervous. "Mars, uh, I don't wanna hear yo' mouth, but I gotta piss now too."

He laughed. "Yeah, I just bet you do. I texted li'l homie behind us to let them know that I'm finna be stopping so I can take a piss. We gon' roll a few more miles before I pull over."

"That's fine."

Mars nodded. He could smell her perfume waft over to him. "Say, Ashley, I wanna say something to you, but I don't want you to get mad, or feel some type of way."

"What's dat?" she asked. She prayed that Mars wasn't trying to come on to her. She didn't feel like shooting his ass down, especially since they were about to embark on a dangerous mission.

"Well, the other day after I left you and Mudman together I didn't leave right away. I was on some nosy shit, and I heard you tell dat nigga dat you was pregnant. Is dat true?"

Ashley felt like her privacy had been invaded. She gave him a look that told him she was disgusted with his antics. She felt like slapping his face. "Mars, what is wrong with you? Isn't eavesdropping a little high school?"

Mars shrugged his shoulders. "I don't give a fuck what it is. I care about you, and I'm not finna sit back and let no nigga hurt you. It's as simple as dat."

She had to piss so bad now that she was fidgeting in her seat. "Well, it ain't none of yo' bidness if I am pregnant. I ain't gon' have the baby anyway," she blurted.

Mars smiled. He liked the sound of that. He didn't want her being hitched to any other man. "Well, I apologize for being nosy, but I just don't trust dude around you. So until things change, I'ma keep yo' best interest at heart." He looked up and saw that he was a mile out from where he was supposed to pull over.

"Mars, I'm thankful for you, but you had your chance with me already. You blew it. I can't ever see myself going backwards. I deserve better than that."

"I don't give a fuck what you say, Ashley. Everybody makes mistakes. I messed up in the past because I was a teenager and I didn't know what I had. Now that I do, I will never fail you again. I'ma treat you like the Queen that I know you are. For your sake and for my daughter's sake. You owe me that." He looked over at her.

Ashley lowered her head. "Why are you at me so hard all of the sudden? You never cared about me in the past. Is it because you see that I am smitten with another man?"

"Yep. I don't want you loving no other nigga but me. We have a child together. It's supposed to be you and me until the end." He began to slow the van down.

"Having a kid doesn't solve everything," she returned.

"Nall, but it gives us a reason to keep fighting for the unit of our family." He pulled the van to the side of the road next to a cornfield.

Ashley took off her seat belt. "You bet' not be looking at me while I pee neither."

Mars got out of the van and came around to open her door. "Take my hand. Dese stalks high as hell."

Ashley smacked his hand away. "Boy, I got it." She climbed out and jumped on to the crunchy grass. "A'ight, where we finna piss at, 'cause I gotta go bad as a muthafucka. I feel like my - "

Mars saw the masked men jump up from across the road. He threw Ashley to the ground and jumped on top of her just as the shooting started.

Boom! Boom! Boom! Boom! Whooooom! The van rocked from side to side as bullet after bullet slammed into the side of it, shattering its windows. The tires deflated. The sounds of the gunfire echoed in the night.

"What is happening?!" Ashley screamed.

"We under attack. Just stay down, baby. I got you. I ain't finna let nobody hurt you," Mars said as the gunfire intensified.

Hood Rich

Chapter 17

Mudman looked up to Mars with the wrath of the devil boiling inside of him. "How much of my muthafuckin' money did you say you lost again?" Mudman was sitting in a big wicker chair inside of the Acorn Project's apartment that he used for his headquarters.

"All of it. A ma'fucka blindsided us. They shot up the van. Rushed us, kilt the three dudes I had on security, and would have killed me and Ashley too had I not jumped on top of her. Mudman, I swear I - "

Mudman kicked him as hard as he could directly in the nuts with both of his feet. "Bitch-ass nigga."

Mars went flying backward He flipped over the table and wound up on his back. He scooted backward on his ass. "Come on, man. What the fuck are you doing?" he asked.

Mudman flipped the table and grabbed the Louisville slugger bat from the side of the couch. "Fuck nigga, you had one job. All you had to do was to get my paper to Sinaloa. You let my shit get took!" He raised the bat and brought it down on to Mars's right leg, breaking the bone.

Mars hollered out in pain. "You son of a bitch." He reached under his shirt and grabbed his pistol.

As soon as he did, the entire room full of Mudman's killas cocked their weapons. They aimed them at Mars. All were ready to blast him away. They refused to allow for him to shoot at Mudman.

"Drop that ma'fuckin' gun, Mars. I don't wanna have the crew do dis to you," Ashley said, feeling some type of way.

Mars frowned and set the gun on the carpet. He winced in excruciating pain. He could see that his bone was sticking out of his leg. "Ashley, tell dis nigga what happened. You was

right there wit' me. Tell him how we was finna use the bathroom in the cornfield, and they bum rushed us. Dat if we would have been in dat truck, that they would have killed us."

"Nigga, it sound like you just told her a whole-ass story. She ain't gotta tell me shit." He looked over to her. "Shawty, you vouching for dis nigga right now?"

Ashley's sweat down the side of her face. She didn't know what to do. She didn't want to say the wrong things and then come out looking like she was on Mars's side. That would have made her an enemy. She knew better. But then again, she had to remember that Mars had just saved her from being gunned down by the enemy. She owed him a bit of loyalty. "Look, Mudman, I don't know what's what, but ma'fuckas did try and kill us. He hopped on top of me while the whole shooting was going down. Dat's all I know."

"See, I told you," Mars said.

Mudman stood over him. "Nigga, I been a jack boy my whole life. I plan wit' da best of dem. You don't thank I know you envy me cause I was fuckin' yo' baby mama?" He pointed at Ashley with the bat.

Mars shook his head. "I ain't sweating dat shit. She gotta make her own decisions. If she wanna fuck wit' you, den it is what it is."

Mudman walked over to Ashley and snatched her necklace off of her. The charm to the gold-plated charm on the necklace was nothing more than a recorder so he could keep tabs on them. "Nigga, I heard everything that you and my li'l young bitch was talking 'bout. You a sucka. You hate me because I'm fuckin' her."

Ashley lowered her head. "Damn, he got you dere."

"Yeah, I do." Mudman stepped up, and swung the bat again. This time he aimed at Mars's head, but he wound up crashing it into his wrist, breaking it.

Mars hollered and jumped up. He hopped on one leg. "Come on, man! Dis is bullshit. I been nothing but loyal to you. So I still got a few feelings for Ashley. So what? Dat's my baby mother. We got history. I'm always gon' love her. That ain't got shit to do wit' me handling my bid-"

CRACK!

Mudman swung the bat and hit him on the side of the head with it, knocking Mars off of his feet and to the ground. "Where the fuck is my money, nigga? You can't outthink me."

Mars crawled around on the floor with blood gushing from his head. He was discombobulated. "I don't know. I swear I don't know."

Ashley felt bad for him. She knew it was a wrap. Once Mudman got to going, she knew that he wouldn't stop until he killed him. Though she felt sorry for Mars, she was ready for him to be out her life anyway. She hated doing the back and forth thing with the drop-offs and pick-ups when it came to their daughter. She simply was cool with raising her on her own. She didn't trust Mars. She thought he was a creep of a man.

"Nigga, where is my money?" Mudman followed him as he crawled around the living room. The crowd of killas backed out of the way.

"Mudman, I ain't got yo' shit." Mars breathed heavily. His face was covered in blood.

Mudman kicked him in the ass. "Nigga, I know how dis game go. You sell the niggas that you don't like to the highest bidder. So who did you sell my lick to, huh? Who are you using to double cross me? You kept insisting on stopping that van to piss. You knew right where to stop. Dat shit ain't by coincidence. You thank I'm stupid?" He kicked him in the ribs and flipped him over.

Mars got back to his knees. Blood was in his eyes. "Mudman, don't do dis shit. I can get yo money back," he mumbled.

"What?" Mudman hadn't heard him clearly.

"He said he can get yo' money back." Ashley helped translate.

Mudman pointed the bat at her. "Shawty, stay in yo' lane. Don't say another muthafuckin' word." He grabbed Mars by the shirt and pulled him up. "You got somethin' you wanna say to me?"

Mars was dizzy. His eyes rolled into the back of his head. "I know who got yo' money, Mudman. I'm sorry."

"Oh, you sorry, huh?" Mudman placed his ear against his bloody lips. "Tell me why you sorry, Mars?"

"'Cause I set da shit up," Mars said in a hoarse voice.

Ashley covered her mouth with her right fist. She knew it was a wrap. There was no way that he was going to be able to walk away from Mudman alive. That just wasn't going to happen.

"So you set me up? Why would you do dat, Mars? Nigga, I got you eating harder than Payroll ever had you eating. You pushing a Lexus, nigga. From what I heard, Payroll had you pushing a punk-ass Nissan. Dis how you do me?" Mudman grabbed him by the throat and squeezed him as hard as he could. "Who got my money?" He choked him until his hand was covered with his blood. Then he let him go, and dropped him to the floor. "Who?"

Mars fought to stand back up. He didn't want Ashley to see him down on the ground like a sucka. He came to his feet, swung, and punched Mudman so hard in the jaw that Mudman dropped the bat. He stumbled backwards. He rushed him, tackling him around the waist. Mudman's shooters were looking for a good shot.

Mudman must have sensed this. "Don't shoot his bitch ass. Don't shoot. I got dis," he assured them. He flipped Mars with a simple hip thrust.

Mars landed on his head. A squirt of blood seeped out. He stood back up and held his guards. "Nike gon' kill yo' bitch ass. Dat's who got yo' money. You want dat shit, go and get it like Tyson."

He swung again. BAM!

Mars felt his head split wide open. He stumbled forward and turned around. He couldn't stop his eyes from going cross. When he focused them, he saw Ashley standing in front of him holding a bat. "Baby?"

Ashley swung the bat with all of her might. She connected with his forehead and knocked him against the wall. He slid down it with his eyes wide open. She rushed to him and beat him senseless for two full minutes. "You don't touch my daddy. You never touch him. I will kill yo' bitch ass." Bam! Bam! Bam! Bam! Over and over until Mars's blood was all over the living room and bystanders.

Mudman sat back, and crossed his legs on the couch while she did her thing. He was already thinking of ways to get at Nike's chin. The treaty had been officially broken. On top of that, he needed to the money back. The deadline for The Bull was in twenty-four hours.

Prentice stepped out into the rain with the deer hunting knife in his right hand. He took three steps and stopped in the middle of the parking lot as the rain came down harder, and harder. His clothes were matted to him within seconds. "Say, fuck nigga, you already know what dis is."

Figgady stopped in his tracks and turned around. When he saw Prentice standing in the middle of the parking lot with a knife in his hand, he clenched his teeth. "Bitch-ass nigga. You killed my daughter." He pointed at him.

"Yep. I murked that li'l bitch. So what you gon do about it, fat boy?"

Figgady took his jacket off. He slung it to the pavement. He thought about rushing to his whip to grab his pistol. He knew he would be able to gun Prentice down before he could get away. But then again, he wanted to savor murdering him. Bullets were too fast.

Prentice laughed. "Nigga, yo' bitch ass followed me all the way to California? Really, and you ain't been shit since you been here. You killed yo' own cousin, and his bitch. I thought I was crazy." Lightning flashed across the sky. Prentice began walking toward him. "So you wanna do dis?"

Figgady held out his hands. "Angola style, baby. Put dat ma'fuckin' knife in the middle of da battlefield, and we square up over here. The first ma'fucka to get to it get to do whatever they wanna do wit' it."

Prentice smiled and nodded his head. He slammed the knife to the ground. "Fuck nigga, you ain't said shit but a word."

Figgady took two big steps, and then he was running at him at full speed. "Bitch-ass nig-GA!" When he got to him he swung as fast and as hard as he could, trying to take Prentice's head off.

Prentice ducked and punched him in the ribs with his right hand. He smacked him across the face with his left. He jumped back laughing. "Nigga, I could have killed you three times tonight. But fuck dat. I wanna relish killing you. You came a long way for dis ass whooping." Prentice squared back up and swung to knock Figgady out.

Cartel Killaz 3

Figgady bear hugged him and bit a plug out of his face. He lifted him all the way in the air and fell on the ground with him, smashing him. "Chicago Bear, nigga!"

Prentice felt his bones crunching. His face stung. Blood went into his ear. No matter how much he tried to get Figgady off of him, he couldn't move. The more he moved himself, the worse off he felt.

Figgady head-butted Prentice in the face and jumped up. "Get yo' bitch ass up. Now!"

Prentice climbed from his knees to his feet. He put up his guards. "Dat's how you want dis shit, huh? Dat's how you wanna do me?" he snapped. He ran at Figgady wildly.

Figgady grabbed him by the throat and lifted him up into the air. He slammed him back to the ground so hard that he knocked the wind out of him. Figgady began stomping him right away.

Prentice couldn't breathe. He struggled to catch his breath. He curled into a ball. He felt Figgady's big foot crush his head to the ground, busting it.

Figgady stopped and picked Prentice up. He lifted him over his head and slammed him down again on the wet pavement. "You killed my baby. She was only a child!" He took off running for the knife.

Prentice struggled to get up. When he got to his feet, he staggered around, loopy. "So, I can't fuck wit' you fighting. Nall, nigga, I ain't never been no scrapper. Dat's why I keep a pistol off in my boxers." He pulled the .380 from his waistband.

Figgady was drunk with rage. By the time he saw the gun, it was too late. He slammed the knife into Prentice's forearm. "Arrgh!"

BOOM! BOOM! BOOM! BOOM!

Prentice held the gun to Figgady's shoulder and popped him four times. He watched Figgady jump back and take off running. He yanked the knife out of his forearm, and threw it to the ground. He pursued him, busting. BOOM! BOOM!

Figgady was running on pure adrenalin. His chest felt like he'd swallowed a ball of fire. He could barely breathe. But he kept running as fast as he could, fighting through the pain.

Prentice was like a track star with blood coming from his arm. When he got close enough to Figgady, he pressed the gun to his back and popped him in the spinal cord. The spark was bright in the dark parking lot.

Figgady took two more steps before his legs locked up on him. He was paralyzed from the waist down immediately. He lay on his stomach, pulling himself across the parking lot.

Prentice had recovered the knife. He hurried back to Figgady and walked along side of him. "There can only be one king of dis shit, Figgady. Just one. You don't know my struggle. You don't know what made me dis way."

Figgady ignored him and kept crawling. He struggled to breathe. He could taste his own blood in his mouth. Flashes of his daughter Chiah came through this mind. Then Chela. He missed them both.

Prentice jumped into the air and brought the knife down as hard as he could into Figgady's back. Then he pulled backward, ripping him down the middle. He raised it again, and repeated the same process.

Figgady felt himself being gutted out from his back. Blood pooled around under his body. He spit up a bloody loogey. It drained out of his nose. He struggled to fight forward. Then he felt Prentice stab the knife into his neck, leaving it there. Prentice stood up and kicked him in the side of the head, snapping it. Figgady was dead before his forehead hit the ground.

Prentice grabbed his knife out of his neck and held it looking down on him.

"One down, two to go."

Hood Rich

Chapter 18

One... Two... Three... WHOOM!

Mudman rushed into the trap house with his Draco leading the way. He saw two dope boys that had been bagging up a kilo of Nike's dope jumping up from the table. Before they could even reach him, held the trigger to his assault rifle and gunned them down with no mercy. The bullets entered into their flesh, and left them riddled on the carpet of the trap. Mudman kept moving forward inside. His shooters moved into overdrive. They popped their pistols beside him, and kept moving forward. The trap house was in utter chaos as the many dope boys tried to make a run for it in every direction. Mudman had already given his troops the order to murder with no regard. They weren't just coming for Nike's stash, and the money he had stolen from Mudman they were coming for blood.

Mudman continued to move through the house with his Draco pressed up against his shoulder. He looked as if he were acting out a military exercise. But this was no exercise. He was on a mission. He kicked open one door after the next. He found the rooms empty. Then he made his way to the back of the house, and up the stairs. His Draco leading the way. Once he got upstairs he crept down the hallway. He slowly came to the first door, and tried the lock.

Locka-locka-locka! Locka-locka-locka! Locka-locka-locka!

Bullets ripped through the door. He jumped backward. More shots were fired. He waited until they ceased, and opened the door jumping back out of the way. He expected to hear more gunshots. When quietness sat in. He jumped in the doorway bussing. Bocka-bocka-bocka! Bocka-bocka-bocka! Bocka-bocka-bocka!

The shooter was caught loading his rifle. Bullets wet up the side of his jaw. Two went through his neck. He felt against the walls and on to his face where he died instantly. Mudman rushed into the room. He searched under the bed. He flipped it over. He pulled open the closet door and jumped back.

Inside of the closet were two buss-downs. They were hood hoes that liked to sit in trap houses and be fucked senseless by multiple dope boys. They screamed as soon as he opened the door. Mudman mugged them. He thought about taking their lives for a seconds, then decided against it. They were of no threat to him. He moved out of the way.

Ashley stepped forward and unloaded on the pair. Her assault rifle jumped in her hands. Shell casings spit into the air and wound up on the carpet. She yanked the women out and searched for anything that could have belonged to Mudman. When she came up empty, she continued to follow Mudman around the house.

Mudman searched each room. He turned them upside down. Two of them were used for a bagging post. When it was all said am done he'd recovered a total of four bricks of Tar and thirty thousand dollars. On an average day, this would have been a good lick. But seeing as he was seven hundred and twenty thousand dollars in debt to the Sinaloa Cartel this was as bad a lick as he could come across. His Intel had been faulty. He was told that the trap would have been the trap that Nike used as his safe house. But it wasn't. Mudman cursed under his breath and punched the wall. "Grab all dat shit. Let's get the fuck out of here.

Later that night, Mudman sat in the dark basement with a shrine in his vein. He pushed down on the dropper and pulled

the rope off of his arm. After it was released, he fed the heroin into his system, and closed his eyes. The drug rushed through his blood stream immediately. He felt numb within seconds. His favorite melody began to play in his ears. He licked his dry lips. "I fucked up. I fucked up, mane. Damn, I fucked up. I should have never trusted dat nigga." He shook his head.

Keisha appeared in the doorway to the basement. "You sitting down here in dis dark ain't gon' help us figure out dis damn situation. Dem cartel boys coming for our ass, and it ain't nothing we can do about it."

"Fuck The Bull. Dat nigga can kiss my ass, shawty. It was all a set-up. Ma'fuckas be thanking dey can win once they get to fucking wit' da Cartel. Well let me tell you now, once dat damn cartel gets involved, you playing a losing game. It's impossible to thrive fucking wit' dem," he slurred. He closed his eyes and dozed off.

Keisha sat across from him and lit a candle. The small flame illuminated the basement. Its flickering light made Mudman look as if he were shaking to her. "Rome, you know we need to get the fuck out of California. When the time runs out on that clock, they are going to kill us. You know that, don't you?"

Mudman nodded for a full minute. He jerked awake. "Dey ain't gon' kill us Keisha. How can dey? We smarter than them, baby. You know we are. Ma'fuckas been trying to kill us since Baton Rouge. But look where we at."

Keisha looked him over. She felt defeated by their situation. But if she knew Mudman like she thought she knew him, she knew that he had to have a trick up his sleeve. "So what is it, baby?"

Mudman opened his eyes and wiped his face with his hand. "What are you talking about?"

"The plan? For as long as I've known you, you've always had a plan. I know you got one dis time too."

Mudman rubbed his nose and sneezed three times in a row. He wiped his mouth on the sleeve of his shirt. Then he laid back on the sofa. "I'm stuck, shawty. They got me. If I get back out there and hustle, I'm not gon' be able to make back The Bull's money before eight o'clock, so he gon' kill me. If he don't, den I got half the killas in Oakland and Los Angeles looking for me. Sooner or later, somebody gon' catch me. If they don't, then maybe the niggas in Baton Rouge done tracked me down. Prentice's bitch ass still out there. The Dominicans from Lawrence. Man, I'm just tired, Keisha. Dis shit done finally whooped my ass. I just wanna sit hurr now and do dis dope. What else is dere to do?"

Keisha cringed. "Fuck you say?" She was so disgusted that she didn't know what to say to him.

"You heard me. I'm tired. It is what it is." He started to get his works ready again.

Keisha stared at him in utter disbelief. "You mean to tell me dat yo monkey ass done brought me dis far to fail me? Aw hell muthafuckin' nawl. Nigga, you got da game all da way fucked up."

Mudman injected another round of the heroin into his system. He shook and squeezed his eyelids as tight has he could. It didn't matter how tight because he couldn't feel it. He nodded out for five minutes. When he opened his eyes again, Prentice was standing behind Keisha with a hockey mask over his face. He held the blade to her neck. The mask smiled at him. He closed his eyes again and opened them. This time Keisha was nowhere to be found. Mudman stood up, and rubbed his face. "Baby. Where are you at?"

Keisha was upstairs on the side of their bed on her knees. She had already said a lengthy prayer to Jehovah. She asked

him for forgiveness over and over again. She prayed that he would deliver them from evil, and wrap them into his holy embrace.

Mudman staggered into the room. "Baby, are you cool in hurr?"

Keisha stood up and nodded. "Nigga, I'm so disgusted with you right now that I honestly don't know what to do." He straightened out the bed. "You remember how Prentice used to be high and fucked up all the time? You remember how he used to smell all foul and shit?"

Mudman nodded. He leaned against the wall so it could hold him up. "Yeah, I remember all dat shit. Why?"

"Because you are the new him." She fluffed the pillow and tossed it on the bed. "You don't have no direction. No drive. No ambition anymore. All you wanna do is get high. I swear I never thought I would see the day." She brushed past him.

"Baby, wait." Mudman reached out for her with his eyes closed.

Keisha jerked away from him, disgusted. "Get the fuck away from me."

There was a knocking on the front door.

Mudman came out of his waistband with his Glock .40. He cocked it and ran to the doorway of the bedroom. "Keisha, get yo' ass in the closet. It could be The Bull."

She smacked her lips. "Nigga, move. Dat is Ashley. She just texted me before I dropped down to pray. She said she was in the area, and she needed to speak with me about something important. So I told her to come on over. Now move." She brushed past him again and went to the front door of townhouse. She peeked through the side window, and saw Ashley standing on the porch with a Chanel book bag on her back.

Keisha took the locks off of the door and opened it. "Hey girl."

Ashley stepped inside and gave Keisha a hug. "I didn't mean to drop by like dis, but you and I gotta talk."

Keisha nodded. "Dat's cool, baby, come on in." She directed her with her arm.

Ashley stepped inside and saw Mudman lurking in the darkness. His gray eyes appeared almost scary in the dimly-lit inside. "Hey, Mudman."

He stepped back into the hallway, and made his way down to the bedroom. He was so high that his heart was beating out of control. He needed to sit down. Once he rested for a second he would be able to think things through thoroughly, he assured himself.

"What's the matter with him?" Ashley asked.

"Don't worry about him. Girl, what do you wanna talk about?" Keisha said, smiling at her. She looked into Ashley's green eyes and suddenly she thought she knew. She felt a cold chill go down her spine. She peeped her green eyes and yellow skin. She tuned into her pretty face, the curves of her body, and she knew that she had been the woman that Mudman had cheated on her with.

"Do you mind if I have a seat on your couch?" Ashley asked, politely.

Keisha shook her head. "No, be my guest."

Ashley took a seat and crossed her thick thighs. Keisha peeped them and grew angry. She saw right away what must have seduced Mudman.

"Okay, Keisha, now before we even begin, I just want to let you know that I respect you, and that I care about you a great deal. I would never do anything into hurt you, or Mudman. I just had to come to you as a woman because - "

"Bitch, how long you been sleeping wit' Mudman?" Keisha interrupted her.

Ashley was taken off guard. "Excuse me?"

"You heard what the fuck I said, li'l girl. How long have you been sleeping with my man behind my back?"

Ashley looked down the hallway to see if Mudman was going to make an appearance again. She suddenly felt a lot of tension coming from Keisha, and it made her nervous. "We only slept around a few times. I want to apologize for that. Like I said before, I never meant to hurt you. I just wanted to come to admit things to you like a woman."

"It's funny how the side bitches always saying that they never wanna hurt the main bitch when in actuality, y'all don't give a fuck about nobody other than yourselves. When was the last time you slept with my man?"

"Been about a week or so. But we've called everything off. And that's not the sole reason why I am here," Ashley started.

"Oh, it just keeps getting better, huh? Well, why don't you go ahead and tell me why you are really here?" Keisha felt her temper getting hot. The more she looked across at Ashley, and gazed over how bad she was, she felt more and more heated. She was imagining Mudman having a field day with the young woman's body.

"Well, you see, during the time that me and Mudman were messing around, I wound up getting pregnant. He is the father. He's the only man that I have been with in almost a year. I'm sorry. I didn't mean for dis to happen. But it did. I'm just hollering at you woman to woman."

Keisha rubbed her hands together, and trained her eyes on a spot on the carpet that she had never noticed before. She was afraid that if she looked directly at Ashley that she was going to do a few things that she regretted. "Ashley, you're not about to have dis baby, are you?"

Ashley nodded her head. "Yeah, I don't believe in abortions. I'm going to have my baby even if I have to take care of it alone."

Keisha was stuck. She felt so tired. So defeated. So pissed off that she didn't know what to do. "Mudman! Get yo' ass in hurr!" she hollered.

It took a moment. Then Mudman appeared out of the dark hallway with his bullet proof vest on. His arms were ripped. Veins decorated both of them. He felt like his head was spinning around on his neck. He gathered himself, and stepped beside Keisha. "Shawty, you already know dat I been fuckin' somebody. Turns out it was her. Let's move on wit' dis bullshit. We gotta bigger thangs to worry about den dis."

Both women were offended at how lightly he was taking the situation. They eyed him with annoyance. The room was quiet. The sound of the air conditioning unit resonated loudly.

Keisha jumped up and smacked him. "Fuckin' is one thang. You bogus fa doing dat behind my back. But now you got dis bitch pregnant. Are you out of your mind?"

Mudman felt his face stinging. Then the pain went away. The heroin took over his system. He wiped the blood that appeared in the corner of his mouth. He looked at his fingers that were coated with it. "Look, shawty, I fucked up. I did what I did. I apologize, and dat's the best I can do."

Keisha pointed into his face. "Nigga, I love you. I love you with all of my heart, but I'll be damned if you play me for a goofy. You and dis bitch better figure dis shit out. She not having dis baby. If you even thank dat's a possibility, I'll kill you and her. Nigga, now try me." She mugged him. Then she glared at Ashley with a murderous stare. "Bitch, you better get yo' shit together, or I swear to God I will murder yo' ass dead. You ain't having his seed. Dat shit ain't happening." Keisha

waved them off. "Y'all fix dis shit." She disappeared into the hallway.

As soon as she stepped into it, Prentice placed the double barrel shotgun to her forehead and placed his finger to his lips. Keisha swallowed. She knew if she screamed that he would blow her away, so instead she held up her hands and followed him to the back of the house.

Chapter 19

"You just had to say something to hurr 'bout dis shit, Ashley? Bitch, I told you dat we was gon' holler at her when da time was right. Ain't nobody tell you to brang yo' monkey ass over hurr wit' dis bullshit tonight. Damn."

Ashley ran her fingers through her hair. "Mudman, why do you always refer to me as a bitch?"

"What da fuck you ask me?" he snapped. The heroin was beginning to wear off of him. His common sense was beginning to kick in.

"You heard what I said. Ever since you and I have been getting down, you have referred to me as a bitch more than you have my name. Now it's one thang if I carried myself any less dan a Queen, but it's another when you seek to disrespect me at every turn for no reason. So answer my question?"

Mudman frowned. "Shawty, ain't nobody got time for dat shit. Long as I been fuckin wit' you, dat's what I been calling you. Now all da sudden you want me to call you somethin different. Bitch, stay in yo' lane."

Ashley sat on the couch and nodded her head. "I'm about to have your baby, Mudman. I'm about to be a mother to your child. That alone should make you stop calling me the bitch word. I'm not a bitch anyway. I been one hunnit to you ever since we been a part of each other. You should have way more love, and respect for me. I mean how many times have I poured my heart out to you? How many times have I slumped a nigga for you?"

Mudman was thrown off. "Shawty, why da fuck is we doing dis lovey dovey shit? You came over hurr tonight on dis bullshit. You got my lady all fucked up in da head. Now I gotta hear her ma'fuckin' mouth. Bottom line is what is we 'bout to do 'bout dis damn baby, mane? I thank we should seriously

revisit the whole you getting rid of it thang." He grabbed his codeine-filled bottled water off of table and turned it up.

"I'm not killing my baby, Mudman. There is nothing that you can say or do to me that would make me harm my child. I know that you and Keisha got history and all of dat, but she don't dictate what happens to mines. I came here because I owed her the truth as a woman. Anythang outside of that both you and her can kiss my ass. Ain't no hoes over hurr. I mean dat." She stood up.

"Bitch, sit yo' ass back down until I tell you to get up," he snapped.

Ashley sat back down without even thinking to defy his orders. "What, Mudman?" She rolled her eyes.

Mudman stood up. He placed his gun on the table, and walked over to her, and squat down. He mugged her for a long time. "Bitch, do you know who I truly am?" he asked in a voice barely above a whisper.

Ashley nodded. "Yep, I know just who you are. I seen you in the streets, Mudman. I seen how you act, and how you control other niggas. I seen you kill ma'fuckas in cold blood, and I done seen you beat a nigga senseless right in front of your whole crew. You are relentless. You're deadly. I can't take dat from you."

"Den why da fuck are you playing wit' me, Ashley? You done brought yo' ass to my home. You done disrupted my family life. All you was supposed to be was my side bitch for da moment. Dis shit wasn't never supposed to spill over into whatever the fuck dis is. So what's your problem?"

"Like I said, I've seen you in all those various stages. But I have also seen you behind the scenes. I've felt how it feels to be alone with you. I've seen the way you look at me when nobody else of around. I've felt the way you have touched me. We've connected on a level far more spiritual than a side

thing. You can't tell me that you have never had any real feelings for me."

"Yes, I can. I've only loved one female in dis world, and that is Keisha. Dat's the love of my life right there. Don't nobody mean shit to me other than her, and there is nothing in dis world that I wouldn't do for or about her."

Ashley stood back up. "Oh, is dat right?"

"Dat's muthafuckin' right," Mudman assured her.

Prentice stepped into the room, clapping his hands. "Bravo. Muthafuckin' bravo. I gotta say, you sound like a real good nigga. Lucky for you, I know better." He held a .45 with a silencer in his hand.

Ashley got up and flipped her hair over her shoulders. "Dis nigga whipped just like you said he is, daddy." She walked up to Prentice and kissed him on the lips.

Prentice tongued her down. He kept his eyes on Mudman the entire time. When he broke the kiss, he smiled into Ashley's green eyes. "You did good, baby. Daddy gon' make sure you good from hurr on out. You hear me?"

"Yes, daddy." She stood behind him and took two .9s from the small of her back. "Mudman, you's goofy."

Two muscle bound security men of Prentice's carried a bound to the chair Keisha into this room. They sat her in the middle of the floor and stepped back. Mudman saw that they were armed. He thought about making a dive for his gun that was on the table.

Before he could, Ashley grabbed it and ran back behind Prentice. "I can read yo' mind, Mudman. You ain't getting dis ma'fucka."

Prentice laughed. "Say, mane, what, you thought you was da one dat turned her into a savage? Nigga, stop playing. I been fucking wit' shawty since she was thirteen. Her mama

and my mama went to da same high school out hurr. You forget that Oakland is where I'm originally from." He shook his head and laughed.

Mudman glanced over to a bound Keisha. His heart felt heavy as a ton of bricks. Then he felt intense anger. "Bitch-ass nigga. You and this turncoat tramp can let my shawty go, and can do whatever you want wit' me. She ain't got shit to do wit' dis."

Ashley cocked her head back. "Ain't got shit to do wit' it? Nigga, please. Ain't dis bitch da one dat cheated on him for you?" Ashley asked.

"Yeah, nigga, she started dis shit. All she had to do was keep her legs closed, but she couldn't even do dat. Now look at her. She thought she was fuckin wit' a winner when all along she was fuckin' a dead nigga," Prentice snarled. He turned and punched a hole in the wall. Then he started to shake. "You two muthafuckas turned me crazy. How da fuck y'all gon' betray me like dat?"

"Nigga, suck dat shit up. Like I said, do whatever you wanna do wit' me, but let Keisha go."

Prentice grabbed Ashley's book bag and pulled a deer hunting knife out of it, the same knife that he had used to kill Figgady. "You say you gon' die for her, right?"

Mudman looked around the room. There were a total of four armed men outside of Ashley and Prentice. He sized them up and thought that he could take them all. He knew he would take a lot of injuries, but he didn't care. All that mattered was that he was able to save Keisha.

Ashley stepped next to Keisha and placed her gun to Keisha's head. She cocked the hammer. "I'll rock-a-bye baby dis bitch if you make one false move. I never liked her black ass. She rubbed me da wrong way. I could tell she always hated me because I looked better than her ass."

"Y'all, tie dis fuck nigga up. I'm finna show you what an autopsy looks like," Prentice jacked.

Mudman took a step back. "Y'all ain't finna do shit to me until you let my woman go."

"Nigga, what? Baby, pop his ass."

Ashley aimed and fired.

BOOM! Her bullet knocked Mudman's knee cap from his leg. He buckled, but remained standing. Blood gushed out of his pants leg and into his shoe. He grimaced. Ashley started laughing.

Prentice joined in. "Karma is a bitch on her period, ain't it?" He motioned for his security to grab an empty chair. They did. "Sit yo' black ugly ass in dat chair right dere. Now, Mudman!"

Mudman remained standing. "Nigga, fuck you. Let Keisha go. I can take whatever I got coming to me. All I'm asking is dat you let her go."

Prentice lowered his eyes. "Aw, so you think that this is a debate, or some kind of a negotiation? Oh, wow." He stepped to Keisha with the deer hunting knife and held it to her throat. "If you don't sit yo' black ass down, I'm finna cut her head off of her shoulders in front of you."

Mudman took a seat. "You a bitch for dis, Prentice."

"Yeah, yeah, yeah, I know. Tie him up," Prentice ordered. His men began binding Mudman to the chair.

"He calls me bitch all the time too, daddy. I think it's just his thing." She laughed.

Prentice nodded. "We gon' see who da bitch is once dis blade get to cutting into his ass."

Once Mudman was bound to the chair, he struggled against his bounds. "Why we can't handle dis shit like men? Let's handle dis shit Angola style."

"Nall, we ain't gon' do dat. I already did dat wit' Figgady. He lost." He cackled and rubbed the side of Keisha's face. He ripped the duct tape off of her face.

Keisha took a deep breath and blew it out. She struggled to get a hold of herself. "Prentice. Stop dis shit. Everybody even around dis ma'fucka."

"Even? Bitch, now you tripping." He grabbed her by the jaw and squeezed it as hard as he could until blood oozed out of her mouth. Then he slapped her.

Keisha spit blood across the room. Mudman tried to break his binds with all of his might. He bounced around in the chair. Ashley laughed like a mental patient.

Prentice held the knife to Keisha's cheek. "Bitch, tell me why you chose dis nigga over me?" He licked her face and stuck his tongue in her ear.

Keisha shivered from disgust. "Stop dat gross-ass shit. I already told you what it was. We ain't finna go through dis shit again," she snapped.

Prentice slowly dragged the blade across her face. A thin trickle of blood seeped out of her wound and ran down her neck. "Tell me, Keisha. Tell me right now, bitch!" He dug the knife deeper. Now the blade was scraping against her bone.

Keisha closed her eyes tight. The pain was unbearable. She could feel her skin ripping like leather. She screamed inside of her head. She refused to give Prentice the satisfaction.

Mudman broke one of the pieces of duct tape and stood up. He was about to rip off the other one when Prentice slid to his right and placed his gun to his temple at the same time he held the knife to Keisha's throat.

"Bitch nigga, make me do it if you want to," Prentice growled.

Mudman froze in place. "You's a bitch, Prentice. You always been a coward ma'fucka. You prey on da weak."

Prentice dropped the knife from against Keisha's throat. "Oh, really?" He raised the gun to Mudman's temple and pulled the trigger three times.

BOOM! BOOM!

Mudman saw two bullets fly out the front of Prentice's face. He fell against him. Mudman pushed him to the ground. Ashley stood over him and aimed at his face. BOOM! BOOM! BOOM! BOOM!

Prentice felt the bullets attacking his face one after the other. His body hopped up and down on the carpet. Brains oozed out of his face and all over his neck. Everything faded to black. His last sight was of Mudman raising his foot to bring not down in the center of his face.

"I couldn't let him kill you like dat, Mudman. I love you way too much. I know dat we meant to be together." She waved her hand, and the security backed out of the room.

Mudman broke his other hand free. He rushed to Keisha's side without so much as an acknowledgment of Ashley. That crushed her soul worse than anything else in life. Mudman ripped Keisha free of her bounds. He wiped the blood away from her cheek. "Are you okay, baby? Huh?"

Keisha nodded. "I am. I'm okay. Thank God for dat."

Ashley watched the way Mudman handled Keisha with tender love and care. It crushed her soul. She couldn't take it anymore. She stood up and began shooting her Draco over and over.

Mudman felt four bullets rip through the back of his neck right away. Big chunks of his flesh flew against the wall. He turned around to face Ashley. She popped him three more times in the forehead. He flew backward, his life leaving him before he even hit the ground.

"Noooooo!" Keisha yelled.

Ashley turned to aim the assault rifle at her. She pulled on the trigger, and it jammed. "Fuck!"

Keisha picked the knife from the floor and rushed her. Ashley turned to run away. Keisha grabbed her long flowing hair, and yanked her backward. She stabbed her in the back of the neck twice. Then she threw her to the ground and straddled her.

"You killed the only man I have ever loved." She slammed her head into the ground, then proceeded to stab her over and over until her right arm gave out. She cried and looked down on her messy body. Ashley lay on her back with her eyes wide open. Her neck looked as if it had been ripped to shreds by an angry lion. Keisha crawled over to a bloody Mudman. She planted a hundred kisses on him. "I love you, baby. I swear to God I do. I will never forget you. I will never forget how you got it in blood."

She jumped up and packed her things. She grabbed the ready-made duffel bag filled with cash, and fled the house out the back door, just as Miguelito, and the Blood Thirsty Cartel assassins kicked in the front. They were on a murderous mission to make Mudman pay what he owed The Bull.

To Be Continued...
Cartel Killaz 4
Coming Soon

Submission Guideline

Submit the first three chapters of your completed manuscript to ldpsubmissions@gmail.com, subject line: Your book's title. The manuscript must be in a .doc file and sent as an attachment. Document should be in Times New Roman, double spaced and in size 12 font. Also, provide your synopsis and full contact information. If sending multiple submissions, they must each be in a separate email.

Have a story but no way to send it electronically? You can still submit to LDP/Ca$h Presents. Send in the first three chapters, written or typed, of your completed manuscript to:

LDP: Submissions Dept
Po Box 870494
Mesquite, Tx 75187

DO NOT send original manuscript. Must be a duplicate.

Provide your synopsis and a cover letter containing your full contact information.

Thanks for considering LDP and Ca$h Presents.

DRUG LORDS II

By **Ghost**

A HUSTLER'S DECEIT III

KILL ZONE **II**

BAE BELONGS TO ME III

SOUL OF A MONSTER III

By **Aryanna**

THE COST OF LOYALTY **III**

By **Kweli**

THE SAVAGE LIFE III

By **J-Blunt**

KING OF NEW YORK V

COKE KINGS IV

BORN HEARTLESS III

By **T.J. Edwards**

GORILLAZ IN THE BAY V

De'Kari

THE STREETS ARE CALLING II

Duquie Wilson

KINGPIN KILLAZ IV

STREET KINGS III

PAID IN BLOOD III

CARTEL KILLAZ IV

Hood Rich

SINS OF A HUSTLA II

ASAD

TRIGGADALE III

Elijah R. Freeman

KINGZ OF THE GAME V

Playa Ray

SLAUGHTER GANG IV

RUTHLESS HEART II

By Willie Slaughter

THE HEART OF A SAVAGE II

By Jibril Williams

FUK SHYT II

By Blakk Diamond

THE DOPEMAN'S BODYGAURD II

By Tranay Adams

TRAP GOD II

By Troublesome

YAYO II

A SHOOTER'S AMBITION II

By S. Allen

GHOST MOB

Stilloan Robinson

KINGPIN DREAMS

By Paper Boi Rari

CREAM

By Yolanda Moore

SON OF A DOPE FIEND II

By Renta

FOREVER GANGSTA II

By Adrian Dulan

LOYALTY AIN'T PROMISED

By Keith Williams

THE PRICE YOU PAY FOR LOVE

By Destiny Skai

THE LIFE OF A HOOD STAR

By Rashia Wilson

TOE TAGZ II

By Ah'Million

Available Now

RESTRAINING ORDER **I & II**

By **CA$H & Coffee**

LOVE KNOWS NO BOUNDARIES **I II & III**

By **Coffee**

RAISED AS A GOON I, II, III & IV

BRED BY THE SLUMS I, II, III

BLAST FOR ME I & II

ROTTEN TO THE CORE I II III

A BRONX TALE I, II, III

DUFFEL BAG CARTEL I II III

HEARTLESS GOON

A SAVAGE DOPEBOY

HEARTLESS GOON I II III

DRUG LORDS

By **Ghost**

LAY IT DOWN **I & II**

LAST OF A DYING BREED

BLOOD STAINS OF A SHOTTA I & II

By **Jamaica**

LOYAL TO THE GAME

LOYAL TO THE GAME II

LOYAL TO THE GAME III

LIFE OF SIN I, II III

By **TJ & Jelissa**

BLOODY COMMAS I & II

SKI MASK CARTEL I II & III

KING OF NEW YORK I II,III IV

RISE TO POWER I II III

COKE KINGS I II III

BORN HEARTLESS I II

By **T.J. Edwards**

IF LOVING HIM IS WRONG…I & II

LOVE ME EVEN WHEN IT HURTS I II III

By **Jelissa**

WHEN THE STREETS CLAP BACK I & II III

By **Jibril Williams**

A DISTINGUISHED THUG STOLE MY HEART I II & III

LOVE SHOULDN'T HURT I II III IV

RENEGADE BOYS I II III IV

By **Meesha**

A GANGSTER'S CODE I &, II III

A GANGSTER'S SYN I II III

THE SAVAGE LIFE I II

By J-Blunt
PUSH IT TO THE LIMIT
By **Bre' Hayes**
BLOOD OF A BOSS **I, II, III, IV, V**
SHADOWS OF THE GAME
By **Askari**
THE STREETS BLEED MURDER **I, II & III**
THE HEART OF A GANGSTA I II& III
By **Jerry Jackson**
CUM FOR ME
CUM FOR ME 2
CUM FOR ME 3
CUM FOR ME 4
CUM FOR ME 5
An **LDP Erotica Collaboration**
BRIDE OF A HUSTLA **I II & II**
THE FETTI GIRLS **I, II& III**
CORRUPTED BY A GANGSTA I, II III, IV
BLINDED BY HIS LOVE
By **Destiny Skai**
WHEN A GOOD GIRL GOES BAD
By **Adrienne**
THE COST OF LOYALTY I II
By Kweli
A GANGSTER'S REVENGE **I II III & IV**
THE BOSS MAN'S DAUGHTERS
THE BOSS MAN'S DAUGHTERS II

Hood Rich

THE BOSSMAN'S DAUGHTERS III

THE BOSSMAN'S DAUGHTERS IV

THE BOSS MAN'S DAUGHTERS **V**

A SAVAGE LOVE **I & II**

BAE BELONGS TO ME I II

A HUSTLER'S DECEIT I, II, III

WHAT BAD BITCHES DO I, II, III

SOUL OF A MONSTER I II

KILL ZONE

By **Aryanna**

A KINGPIN'S AMBITON

A KINGPIN'S AMBITION **II**

I MURDER FOR THE DOUGH

By **Ambitious**

TRUE SAVAGE

TRUE SAVAGE II

TRUE SAVAGE **III**

TRUE SAVAGE **IV**

TRUE SAVAGE **V**

TRUE SAVAGE **VI**

DOPE BOY MAGIC

MIDNIGHT CARTEL

By **Chris Green**

A DOPEBOY'S PRAYER

By **Eddie "Wolf" Lee**

THE KING CARTEL **I, II & III**

By **Frank Gresham**

THESE NIGGAS AIN'T LOYAL **I, II & III**

By **Nikki Tee**

GANGSTA SHYT **I II &III**

By **CATO**

THE ULTIMATE BETRAYAL

By **Phoenix**

BOSS'N UP **I , II & III**

By **Royal Nicole**

I LOVE YOU TO DEATH

By Destiny J

I RIDE FOR MY HITTA

I STILL RIDE FOR MY HITTA

By **Misty Holt**

LOVE & CHASIN' PAPER

By **Qay Crockett**

TO DIE IN VAIN

SINS OF A HUSTLA

By **ASAD**

BROOKLYN HUSTLAZ

By **Boogsy Morina**

BROOKLYN ON LOCK I & II

By **Sonovia**

GANGSTA CITY

By **Teddy Duke**

A DRUG KING AND HIS DIAMOND I & II III

A DOPEMAN'S RICHES

HER MAN, MINE'S TOO I, II

Hood Rich

CASH MONEY HO'S
By Nicole Goosby
TRAPHOUSE KING **I II & III**
KINGPIN KILLAZ I II III
STREET KINGS I II
PAID IN BLOOD **I II**
CARTEL KILLAZ I II III
By **Hood Rich**
LIPSTICK KILLAH **I, II, III**
CRIME OF PASSION I II & III
By **Mimi**
STEADY MOBBN' **I, II, III**
By **Marcellus Allen**
WHO SHOT YA **I, II, III**
SON OF A DOPE FIEND
Renta
GORILLAZ IN THE BAY **I II III IV**
DE'KARI
TRIGGADALE I II
Elijah R. Freeman
GOD BLESS THE TRAPPERS I, II, III
THESE SCANDALOUS STREETS I, II, III
FEAR MY GANGSTA I, II, III
THESE STREETS DON'T LOVE NOBODY I, II
BURY ME A G I, II, III, IV, V
A GANGSTA'S EMPIRE I, II, III, IV
THE DOPEMAN'S BODYGAURD

Tranay Adams

THE STREETS ARE CALLING

Duquie Wilson

MARRIED TO A BOSS... I II III

By Destiny Skai & Chris Green

KINGZ OF THE GAME I II III IV

Playa Ray

SLAUGHTER GANG I II III

RUTHLESS HEART

By Willie Slaughter

THE HEART OF A SAVAGE

By Jibril Williams

FUK SHYT

By Blakk Diamond

DON'T F#CK WITH MY HEART I II

By Linnea

ADDICTED TO THE DRAMA I II III

By Jamila

YAYO

A SHOOTER'S AMBITION

By S. Allen

TRAP GOD

By Troublesome

FOREVER GANGSTA

By Adrian Dulan

TOE TAGZ

By Ah'Million

BOOKS BY LDP'S CEO, CA$H

TRUST IN NO MAN

TRUST IN NO MAN 2

TRUST IN NO MAN 3

BONDED BY BLOOD

SHORTY GOT A THUG

THUGS CRY

THUGS CRY 2

THUGS CRY 3

TRUST NO BITCH

TRUST NO BITCH 2

TRUST NO BITCH 3

TIL MY CASKET DROPS

RESTRAINING ORDER

RESTRAINING ORDER 2

IN LOVE WITH A CONVICT

Coming Soon

BONDED BY BLOOD 2

BOW DOWN TO MY GANGSTA

CPSIA information can be obtained
at www.ICGtesting.com
Printed in the USA
LVHW020216240421
685385LV00005B/552